WELSH TALES OF TERROR

WELSH
Tales of Terror

Edited by R. Chetwynd-Hayes

Collins

FONTANA BOOKS

First published by Fontana Books 1973
Second impression May 1975
Third impression May 1979

Made and printed in Great Britain by
William Collins Sons & Co Ltd, Glasgow

CONTENTS

ACKNOWLEDGEMENTS

The Editor gratefully acknowledges permission to reprint copyright material to the following:

Glyn Jones and J. M. Dent & Sons Ltd. for CADI HUGHES and JORDAN, from *Selected Short Stories by Glyn Jones.*

John Christopher and David Higham Associates Ltd. for A CRY OF CHILDREN. The Estate of the late Arthur Machen and A. M. Heath & Co. Ltd. for THE SHINING PYRAMID.

Angus Wilson and James Barrie Ltd. for ANIMALS OR HUMAN BEINGS.

London Mystery Magazine for THE MORGAN TRUST.

Dennis Dobson for BE THIS HER MEMORIAL by Caradoc Evans, from *My People.*

Mrs. Hazel F. Looker for THE LOST GOLD MINE, © 1972.

Miss Dorothy K. Haynes for MRS. JONES, © 1972.

Ronald Seth and The Hamlyn Publishing Group, Ltd., for THE REVEREND JOHN JONES AND THE GHOSTLY HORSEMAN.

Jack Griffith and Pan Books Ltd. for THE BLACK GODDESS, from *Tales of Unease*; edited by John Burke.

Richard Hughes and Chatto & Windus Ltd. for THE STRANGER, from *Welsh Short Stories* and *A Moment of Time.*

London Management for LORD DUNWILLIAM AND THE CWN ANNWN, © 1972 by R. Chetwynd- Hayes.

EDITOR'S NOTE

Every effort has been made to trace the owners of the copyright material in this book. It is the editor's belief that the necessary permissions from publishers, authors and authorised agents have been obtained, but in case of any question arising as to the use of any material, the editor, while expressing regret for any errors, will be pleased to make the necessary correction in future editions of the book.

INTRODUCTION

I had a good deal of fun when compiling this anthology of Welsh Tales of Terror, although the task was not an easy one.

The Principality is rich in folk-lore and has more than its fair share of ghosts – in fact, so far as I can see, one cannot walk down a country lane after sunset without encountering a headless horseman or a pack of hell-hounds on the rampage. My difficulty lay in selecting from a mass of material an assorted collection that dealt with the many aspects of Welsh supernatural life.

I have chosen two stories by Glyn Jones, *Cadi Hughes* and *Jordan*. *Jordan* has very nice beginning. I quote:

'I am worried. Today when I cut my chin with my white-handled razor I didn't bleed.'

This, understandably, arrested my attention. On the other hand, *Cadi Hughes* has an opening that deals a paralysing blow to the senses, before reviving us with a pulse-stirring twinge of horror.

Upstairs in number one Colliers's Row, Ifan Cariad was dying by inches. People often say 'dying by inches' without really meaning it, but as a description of Ifan it was almost literally true; because his left leg was gangrenous to the knee . . .

Then yesterday two of his toes had come off into her apron . . .

Do you see what I mean?

The terror in John Christopher's *A Cry of Children* does not become apparent until the very end. Then one says 'Of course' with a self-satisfied, if somewhat wry smile, before pondering on the dark currents that run under the most placid stream.

The late Arthur Machen was a most prolific writer. His translation of the *Memoirs Of Casanova*, which ran into six fat volumes, could well have been a life's work for the normal man, but he has left us a rich fund of ghost and supernatural stories as well. *The Shining Pyramid* is set against a Welsh background and tells of the ancient horror that lies beneath the eternal hills. It is beautifully written and grips one's attention from beginning to end.

There is a moral buried somewhere in *Animals or Human Beings* by Angus Wilson; if you are a stranger to these shores, think twice before taking a post as housekeeper in Wales. A fondness for animals is all very well, but . . .

The Morgan Trust by Richard Bridgeman is the kind of supernatural story I most like. I found it in a 1961 copy of *London Mystery Magazine*, and decided it must go into this anthology, even though perhaps the word 'terror' should be replaced by 'apprehension'. It deals with the unseen refuge, the long-sought-for place that lies beyond the mists, that every imaginative writer likes to tackle at least once in his career.

Water-Horses and Spirits of the Mist is not strictly speaking a story at all. I have lifted it from *Folk-Lore and Folk-Stories of Wales* by Marie Trevelyan, and it is a matter of great regret that I cannot trace the passing of this lady or her publishers. Elliot Stock, formerly of Paternoster Row, London E.C. disappeared around 1937 and it is as though they had never existed. I have included this extract because it gives one a marvellous account of the evil monstrosities that have bedevilled Wales since the first Taffy muttered 'Indeed to goodness' at his mother's knee.

Be This Her Memorial by Caradoc Evans is a grand little snippet of Welsh terror; it is of course a first-rate story as well, stressing the hypocrisy that underlines life in a small, religion-bound community. You may well be undecided whether to scream or cry.

The Lost Gold Mine is Hazel F. Looker's first attempt at this kind of fiction, and she has made good use of her knowledge of Welsh folk-lore and pony-trekking. She tells me this story is based on fact, for many people have claimed to have seen the ghost-ponies.

Dorothy K. Haynes, whose story *The Head* appeared in *Scottish Tales of Terror*, wrote *Mrs Jones* specially for this collection. Beware, all you ladies who lust after culinary glory; you may end up like the lamented Mrs Jones – toiling over a hot stove for all eternity.

I am delighted to state that *The Reverend John Jones and the Ghostly Horseman* by Ronald Seth is perfectly true. It is very pleasant for a horrormonger like myself when he can rip aside the comforting curtain called fiction and say 'This really happened, and by golly it could happen to you.' Imagine having a ghostly motorist keeping pace with you down the M.1.

The Black Goddess by Jack Griffith takes place in a coal mine, and was recently made into a television play. Again I was struck by the beginning.

Dill Rees was mad.

Iestyn Morgan had suspected it for a long time; now he was sure of it.

With an opening like that one has to read on.

I have always believed that the horror story should be blended with humour, and Richard Hughes in *The Stranger* has done just that. The little devil that squats in a nest of hot coals is a glorious conception.

Lastly my own contribution, *Lord Dunwilliam and the Cwn Annwn*, grew out of the legend of King Arawn and the Hell-Hounds. I hope you like it.

Following the usual practice with this series I have inserted little chilly snippets between each story, gathered from a fairly wide field. Look upon them as glasses of rather dry wine served between fifteen courses of a very grim banquet. They may help mental digestion.

I would like to take this opportunity of thanking Mrs Olwen Caradoc Evans of Perllan Caradoc, Conway, for her very kind help, loan of many valuable books, and advice, which have helped me in no small measure with the compiling of this anthology.

R. Chetwynd-Hayes.

JORDAN

GLYN JONES

I am worried. Today when I cut my chin with my white-handled razor I didn't bleed. That was the way Danny's shaving went. Danny was my friend. Together we had a spell working the fairs and markets out there in that country where there are nothing but farms and chapels. It was a sort of uncivilised place. I had invented a good line, a special cube guaranteed to keep the flies off the meat, and Danny had his little round boxes of toothpaste. This toothpaste he scraped off a big lump of wet batter, a few pounds of it, greenish in colour and with a bad smell, it stood on a tin plate and sometimes Danny would sell it as corn cure. So as to gather a crowd around his trestle he used to strip down to his black tights and walk about with a fifty-six pound solid iron weight hanging by a short strap from his teeth. This was to show what wonderful teeth you would have if you used Danny's toothpaste. It was only when he was doing this that you ever saw any colour in Danny's face. The colour came because he did the walking about upside down, he was on his hands doing it with his black stockings in the air.

Danny was thin and undersized. If I made a joke about his skinny legs he would lower his lids offended and say, 'Don't be so personal.' He was very touchy. His tights were coms dyed black and they looked half empty, as though large slices had been cut off from inside them. He had a fine, half-starved face, very thin and leathery, like a sad cow. There was only one thing wrong with his face and that was the ears. Danny's ears were big and yellow, and they stood out at right angles to his head. From the front they looked as though they had been screwed into his skull, and one had been screwed in a lot farther than the other. His straight carrot hair was very long and thick and brushed back over his head. When he scuffled about on his bandy arms with that half hundredweight dangling from his teeth, his mop opened downwards off his scalp as though it was on a hinge, and bumped along the cobblestones. He was very proud of his teeth. He thought so much of them he never showed them to anyone. Nobody ever saw Danny grinning.

My own line was that special cube I had invented to keep the flies off the meat. I used to soften down a few candles and shape the grease into dices with my fingers. Then I put one or two of these white dices on a cut of meat on my trestle in the middle of the market crowds. There were always plenty of fat flies and bluebottles buzzing about in those markets, what with the boiled sweet stalls and the horse-droppings, but you never saw one perching on my meat with the white cubes on it. This wasn't because the flies didn't like candle-grease but because under the meat-plate I had a saucer of paraffin oil.

One night Danny and I were sitting on the bed in our lodging house. The place was filthy and lousy and we were catching bugs on our needles off the walls and roasting them to death one by one in the candle flame. Danny was bitter. The fair had finished but the farmers had kept their hands on their ha'pennies. And the weather was bad, very wet and gusty and cold all the time. Danny said we were pioneers. He said these farmers were savages, they didn't care about having filthy teeth, or eating their food fly-blown. He was very downhearted. He hadn't had much to eat for a few days and between the noisy bursting of the bugs his empty belly crowed. I was down-hearted too. We had to get money from somewhere to pay for our lodgings and a seat in the horsebrake drawing out of town the next morning. I asked Danny to come out into the town to see what we could pick up but he wouldn't. At first he said it was too cold. Then he said he had got to darn his tights and his stockings. In the end I went by myself.

The town had been newly wetted with another downpour and Danny was right about the cold. As I walked up the dark empty main street I could feel the wind blowing into the holes in my boots. Everywhere was closed up and silent and deserted.

I looked in at the Bell and the Feathers and the Glyndwr, but they were all empty. Then from the swing door of the Black Horse I saw inside a big broad-shouldered man sitting down by himself in the bar. Apart from him the bar was deserted. He was by the fire and his back was towards me. I knew bumming a drink out of him would be as easy as putting one hand in the other. I knew this because he had a red wig on coming down over the collar of his coat, and a man who wears a wig is lonely.

On the table in front of the man I could see a glass of whisky and in his hand was a little black book. He was singing a hymn out of it in Welsh. It was sad, a funeral hymn, but very determined. I stood by the door of the empty bar and listened. The man seemed huge in the neck and across the shoulders, and every time he moved all the flesh on him seemed to begin to tremble. If he kept dead still he stopped trembling. I went in past him and stood the other side of the table by the fire.

When I got round to the front of this man something snapped like a carrot inside me. His face was hideous. The flesh of it looked as though it had been torn apart into ribbons and shoved together again anyhow back on to the bones. Long white scars ran glistening through the purple skin like ridges of gristle. Only his nose had escaped. This was huge and dark and full of holes, it curved out like a big black lump of wood with the worm in it. He was swarthy, as though he was sitting in a bar of shadow, and I looked up to see if perhaps a roof-beam had come between him and the hanging oil-lamp lighting the bar. There wasn't a hair on him, no moustache or eyebrows, but his wig was like the bright feathers of a red hen. It started a long way back, half-way up his scalp, and the gristly scars streamed down over his forehead and cheekbones from under it. He had a tidy black suit on and a good thick-soled boot with grease rubbed in. The other leg was what looked like a massive iron pipe blocked up at the end with a solid wooden plug. It came out on to the hearth from the turn-up of his trousers

It is best to tell the tale when you haven't got any cash to put on the counter. When I began to talk to him by the fire I tucked my feet under the settle and said I was a salesman. Although Danny and I could put all our belongings in a tobacco-box, I soon had a fine range of second-hand goods for sale. The man closed his little book to listen. He told me he was Jordan, man-servant to the old doctor of the town. I took a polished piece of a rabbit's backbone out of my waistcoat pocket and passed it over to him. It looked like a small cow's skull, complete with horns. He examined it slowly, trembling all the time. He had huge soft hands and his finger-nails were as green as grass. I told him he could keep it. He called for whisky for both of us.

As I drank my whisky I enjoyed thinking what I had for sale. I had a little harmonium, portable, very good for Welsh hymns, perfect except for a rip in the bellows; a new invention that would get a cork out of a bottle – like that! ; a nice line in leather purses, a free gift presented with each one – a brass watch-key, number eight, or a row of glass-headed pins; a pair of solid leather knee-boots, just the thing for him because they were both for the same leg. The man's eyes were small, they looked half closed up, and he watched me hard without moving them all the time. In the heat of the fire a strong smell came off him. It was a damp clinging smell, clammy, like the mildewed corner of some old church, up there behind the organ where they keep the bier. At last he bent forward and held his smashed face close to mine. I stopped talking. He trembled and said softly, 'I am interested in buying only one thing.'

Somehow I felt mesmerised, I couldn't say anything. I am not often like that. I lifted my eyebrows.

Jordan didn't answer. His little eyes slid round the empty bar. Then he moved his lips into a word that staggered me. I stared at him. For a minute by the blazing bar fire I went cold as clay. He nodded his head and made the same mouthing of his smashed face as before. The word he shaped out was, 'Corpses'.

There was dead silence between us. The clock in the bar echoed loudly, like a long-legged horse trotting down an empty street. But I let my face go into a twist and I squeezed a tear into the end of my eye. I crossed myself and offered the serving man the body of my brother. I had buried him, I remembered, a week ago come tomorrow.

Jordan took his hat and stick out of the corner. The stick was heavy, with a lot of rope wound round it, and the black hat had a wide brim. When he stood up he was like a giant rising above me. He was much bigger even than I thought. He looked down hard at the little bone I had given him and then threw it on the back of the fire. We went out into the street. As we walked along, his iron leg bumped on the pavement and made a click-clicking noise like a carried bucket. He would show me where to bring the corpse and I was to come between midnight and daybreak.

We walked together out of the town into the country. It was pitch dark and soon the way was through wet fields. It was still cold but I didn't feel it any more. Jordan had this peg leg but he was big, and I sweated keeping up with him. He trembled all the time as he walked but his shaking didn't make you think he was weak. He was like a powerful machine going full force and making the whole throbbing engine-house tremble to the foundations with its power. I trotted behind him breathless. He was so busy singing the Welsh burial hymn that he didn't drop a word to me all the way.

At last we came to a gate across the lane we were following. There was a farm-house beyond it, all in darkness. Jordan stopped singing and shouted, twice. There was no reply. He started singing again. He poised himself on his iron leg and his walking stick and gave the gate a great kick with his good foot. It fell flat. We found ourselves going at full speed across a farmyard. A heavy sheepdog ran out of the shadows barking and showing a fringe of teeth. He looked huge and fierce enough to tear us in pieces. Jordan didn't pause and I kept close behind him. The dog changed his gallop into a stiff-legged prowl, and he filled his throat with a terrible snarl.

Then suddenly he sprang straight at Jordan's throat. As he rose in the air Jordan hit him a ringing crack on the head with his stick. He used both hands to bring it down. The dog dropped to the pebbles of the yard passing a contented sigh. He didn't move again. Jordan put his good foot on him and brought the stick down on his head again and again. He went on doing this, his sad hymn getting louder and louder, until the dog's brains came out. I went cold in my sweat to hear him. At last he wiped the handle of the stick in the grass of the hedge and went on down the lane, singing.

We came in sight of the lights of a big house. 'That's the place,' he said. 'Bring it round to the back door. Good night.'

He went off into the darkness like a giant in his broad-brimmed hat. I wiped the sweat off my head. After he had disappeared I could hear his hymn and his leg clicking for a long time. His hymn was slow and sad, but it didn't make me unhappy at all. It frightened the life out of me.

On the way back to the town I kicked the dead dog into the ditch.

Danny never let his job slide off his back. As I climbed up the stairs of our lodging house I came face to face with two eyes watching me through the upright bars of the top landing banister. It was Danny dawdling about on his hands, practising. I had a lot of trouble persuading him to be a corpse. All he had to do was pretend to be dead and to let me and the blackman on the landing below carry him out to the doctor's house. Then when we were paid and everybody in the house was asleep he could get out of one of the downstairs windows. We would be waiting for him. We could leave the town by the first brake in the morning. It was safe as houses. Nothing could go wrong. At last Danny agreed.

At midnight the three of us set out for Jordan's house. We were me, Danny and Marky. Marky was a half-caste cheapjack, a long thin shiny man the colour of gunmetal, selling fire-damaged remnants and bankrupt stock and that. He used to dribble and paw you at close quarters but he would do anything you asked him for tuppence or thruppence. We walked through the fields carrying a rolled up sack and my trestle until we came in sight of the house Jordan had shown me. Danny stripped to his coms under a tree and hid his clothes. He put on an old cream-flannel nightgown Marky had brought out of stock. Then we sewed him in the sack and put him on the planks of my trestle. It was pitch dark and cold, with the small rain drizzling down again as fine as pepper.

The doctor's house was all in darkness. We went round to the little pointed wooden door at the back of the garden. I whispered to Danny to ask if he was all right. There were two answers, Danny's teeth chattering and the uproar of dogs howling and barking inside the garden. I had never thought about dogs. What were we going to do?

At once I heard the click of the leg the other side of the wall and Jordan's voice speaking. 'Down, Farw. Down, Angau,' he growled. The narrow pointed door was thrown open, and suddenly we saw Jordan. He was stripped naked to the half and he had left off his wig. He looked so huge, so powerful and ugly in the doorway, with his swelling nose and his fleshy body all slashed, I almost let go of our load with fright. And behind him the hounds, three of them, black and shaggy and big as ponies, yelped and bayed and struggled to get past him to attack us. Jordan spoke sharply to them and at last we were able to carry Danny into the garden. He was as light on the boards as a bag of hay. Jordan spoke only to the dogs. He made a sign and led us hobbling along the pebble path across the yard towards some dark out-houses. The three hounds paced whining beside us, sniffing all the time at the sack and spilling their dribble.

The room we went into smelt like a stable. It was dim and empty but there was an oil-lamp hanging from a nail in a low beam. We laid Danny across some feed-boxes under this lamp. Jordan stood back by the stable door with the whimpering dogs while we were doing it, watching us all the time. I could feel his eyes burning into my back. His skin was very dark and his chest bulged up into big paps resting above his powerful folded arms. But all his body was torn with terrible wounds like his face. Long shining scars like the glistening veins you see running through the rocks of a cliff-face spread in all directions over his flesh. His bald head had a large dome on it and that was covered with scars too. His whole body gleamed down to his waist, the drizzle had given him a high shine like the gloss of varnish.

We left Danny lying on the boards across the feed-boxes and came back up to the door to ask for our money. Jordan didn't reply. Instead he took a large clasp-knife out of the pocket in the front of his trousers and opened it. Then, ordering the dogs to stay, he went past us and bumped over to where Danny was lying in his sack. He seemed to take a long time to get there. There was dead silence. As he went from us we could see a black hole in his back you could put your fist into. My skin prickled. Marky's eyes rolled with the dogs sniffing him and he began to paw the air. I looked round and saw a hay-fork with a stumpy leg in the corner. Jordan turned round under the lamp and looked back at us. The blade of the open knife trembled in his hand. He turned again and cut open the sewing in the sack above Danny's face. I could hardly breathe. Danny was so white under the hanging lamp I thought he was really dead. My hair stirred. Danny's teeth showed shining in his open mouth, and in the lamplight falling right down upon them the whites of his half-opened eyes glistened. He was pale and stiff, as if he had already begun to rot. Jordan bent over, gazing down at him, with the knife in his hand, the lamp spreading a shine over the skin of his wet back. I was frightened, but if Danny's teeth chattered or his belly crowed I was willing to use that pitchfork to get us out. At last Jordan turned. He spoke for the first time.

'He is a good corpse,' he said.

'He is my brother,' I told him.

'Where did you get him from?'

'I dug him up.'

He nodded. He left the knife open on the feed-box and came over to us. Putting his hand again into his front pocket he brought out a large lump of wadding. This he opened and in the middle lay three gold sovereigns. He passed the coins over to me with his huge trembling hands and motioned us out roughly. He went back and blew out the oil-lamp and we left Danny alone there in the darkness. Jordan locked the stable door and the hounds trotted round us growling as we left the garden through the little door.

'Good night,' said Jordan.

'Good night, brother,' I said.

We walked about in the fields, trying to keep warm, waiting for the time to go back to get Danny out. Marky had gone icy cold. I was worried, especially about those dogs. I wished I had a drop of drink inside me. When we thought everything would be quiet again we went back to see if it was safe to give Danny the whistle. I threw my coat over the bottle-glass stuck on top of the garden wall and climbed up. I could see a candle lit in a downstairs window of the doctor's house and by its light Jordan moved about inside the room in his nightshirt and nightcap. Presently his light disappeared and all was in darkness.

An owl in a tree close by started screeching. Marky was frightened and climbed up on to the garden wall to be near me. There was no sign of Jordan's dogs in the garden. It was bitterly cold up there on top of the wall without our coats on. The wind was lazy, it went right through us instead of going round. It had stopped raining again. There was a moon now but it was small and a long way off, very high up in the sky, and shrunken enough to go into your cap.

We waited a long time shivering and afraid to talk. Marky's eyes were like glass marbles. At last I saw something moving in the shadows by the stable. My heart shot up hot into my throat. Marky caught hold of me trembling like a leaf. A figure in white began to creep along the wall. It was Danny. He must have got out through one of the stable windows. I whistled softly to him and at that there was uproar. The three hounds came bounding across the yard from nowhere, making straight for Danny, baying and snarling like mad. I didn't know what to do for the moment with fright. The dogs were almost on top of him. Danny sprang on to his hands and began trotting towards them. His black legs waved in the air and his nightshirt fell forward and hung down to the ground over his head. The dogs stopped dead when they saw him. Then they turned together and galloped away into the shadows howling with fright. When Danny reached the wall we grabbed him firmly by the ankles and pulled him up out of the garden at one pluck. We were not long getting back to our lodging house. The next morning we paid our landlord and the brake driver with one of the sovereigns we had had off Jordan.

I didn't have any luck. All the rest of the summer it was still wet and there were hardly any flies. I tried selling elephant charms, very lucky, guaranteed, but the harvest failed and in the end I couldn't even give them away. Danny got thinner and thinner and more quiet. He was like a rush. He had nothing to say. There never was much in his head except the roots of his hair. Having been a corpse was on his mind. And he was like a real corpse to sleep with, as cold as ice and all bones. He lost interest even in standing on his hands.

We visited a lot of the towns that held fairs but without much luck. One market day we were sitting in a coffee tavern. It was a ramshackle place built of wooden planks put up for the market day in a field behind the main street. The floor was only grass and the tables and benches stood on it. You could get a plate of peas and a cup of tea there cheap. Danny didn't care about food now even when we had it. Because it was market day this coffee tavern was crowded. It was very close inside, enough to make you faint, and the wasps were buzzing everywhere. All the people around us were jabbering Welsh and eating food out of newspapers.

Presently, above the noise, I heard a bumping and clicking sound in the passage. I felt as though a bath-full of icy water had shot over me inside my clothes. I looked round but there was no way of escape. Then I heard the funeral hymn. In a minute Jordan was standing in the entrance of the coffee tavern. He was huge, bigger than ever, a doorful. In one hand was his roped-up stick and in the other his black hymn-book. His broad-brimmed hat was on his head, but instead of his wig he had a yellow silk handkerchief under it with the corners knotted. He stopped singing and stood in the doorway looking round for an empty seat. A man from our table just then finished his peas and went out. Jordan saw the empty place and hobbled in. We couldn't escape him. He came clicking through the eating crowd like an earthquake and sat down at our table opposite us.

At first I didn't know what to do. Danny had never seen Jordan and was staring down at the grease floating on his tea. I tried to go on leading the peas up to my mouth on my spoon but I could hardly do it. Jordan was opposite, watching me. He could see I was shaking. I pretended to fight the wasps. I could feel his bright bunged-up eyes on me all the time. He put his arms in a ring on the table and leaned over towards me. I was spilling the peas in my fright. I couldn't go on any longer. I lowered my spoon and looked at him. He was so hideous at close quarters I almost threw up. The big black block of his nose reached out at me, full of worm-holes, and the rest of his face looked as though it had been dragged open with hooks. But he was smiling.

'Jordan,' I said, although my tongue was like a lump of cork. 'Mr Jordan.'

He nodded. 'You've come back,' he said. 'Where have you been keeping?'

The whole coffee tavern seemed to be trembling with his movements. I felt as though I was in the stifling loft of some huge pipe-organ, with the din coming out full blast and all the hot woodwork in a shudder. His question had me stammering. I told him I had been busy. My business kept me moving, I travelled about a lot. The wooden building around me felt suffocating, airless as a glasshouse. I glanced at Danny. He looked as though he had been tapped and all his blood run off. Even his yellow ears had turned chalky.

Jordan nodded again, grinning his terrible grin. 'The chick

born in hell returns to the burning,' he said. All the time he watched me from under the front knot of his yellow handkerchief. He ignored Danny altogether. His eyes were small, but they looked as though each one had had a good polish before being put into his head.

'Our bargain was a good one,' he went on, still smiling. 'Very good. It turned out well.'

I was afraid he would hear my swallow at work, it sounded loud even above the jabbering. 'I am glad,' I said, 'I did my best. I always do my best.'

'My master was pleased,' he said. He leaned farther forward and beckoned me towards him. I bent my head to listen and his wooden nose was up touching my ear. 'A splendid corpse,' he whispered. 'Inside, a mass of corruption. Tumours and malignant growths. Exactly what my master needed. Cut up beautifully, it did.'

There was a loud sigh from Danny. When I turned to look at him he wasn't there. He had gone down off his bench in a heap on the grass. People all round got up from their tables and crowded round. Some of them waved their arms and shouted. 'Give him air,' they said, 'he's fainted. Give him air.' For a minute I forgot all about Jordan. I told the people Danny was my friend. They carried him out of the coffee tavern and laid him on the grass at the side of the road. 'Loosen his neck,' somebody said, and his rubber breast and collar were snatched off showing his black coms underneath. The crowd came on like flies round jam. At last Danny opened his eyes. Someone brought him a glass of water out of the coffee tavern. He sat up, bowed his shoulders and put his hands over his face as though he was crying. I spotted something then I had never noticed before. There was a big bald hole in his red hair at the top of his head. He looked sickly. But before long he could stand again. I pushed his breast and collar into my pocket and took him back to our lodging house. I looked round but I couldn't see Jordan at all in the crowd. Danny was in bed for a week. He was never the same again. For one thing if he cut himself shaving he didn't bleed. The only thing that came out of the cut was a kind of yellow water.

Before the year was out I had buried Danny. It was wild weather and he caught a cold standing about half-naked in his tights in the fairs and markets. He took to his bed in our lodgings. Soon he was light-headed and then unconscious. Every night I sat by him in our bedroom under the roof with the candle lit listening to his breathing.

One night I dropped off to sleep in the chair and he woke me up screaming. He dreamt Jordan was trying to chop his hands off to make him walk on the stumps. I was terrified at the noise he made. The candle went out and the roar of the wind sawing at the roof of the house was deafening. My heart was thumping like a drum as I tried to relight the candle. I couldn't stop Danny screaming. A few minutes later he died with a yell. Poor Danny. Being a corpse was too much for him. He never struggled out from under the paws of his memories.

The next night the man from the parish came. He asked me if I wasn't ashamed to bury my friend like that. He meant that Danny hadn't had a shave for a week. In the candle-light he had a bright copper beard and he wasn't quite so much like a cow. When the man had gone I started to shave the corpse. It was hard doing it by candle-light. High up on the cheek-bone I must have done something wrong, I must have cut him, because he opened one of his eyes and looked hard at me with it. I was more careful after that. I didn't want to open that vein they say is full of lice.

The morning of the funeral I borrowed a black tie off our landlord. I bummed a wreath on strap. It was very pretty. It was a lot of white flowers on wires made into the shape of a little arm-chair. In the bars of the back was a card with the word 'Rest' on it done in forget-me-nots. Danny always liked something religious like that.

There was nobody in the funeral except the parson and me and two gravediggers. It was a bad day in autumn and very stormy. The long grass in the graveyard was lying down smooth under the flow of the wind. There were some willow trees around the wall all blown bare except for a few leaves sticking to the thin twigs like hair-nits. The parson in his robes was a thin man but he looked fat in the wind. As he gabbled the service the big dried-up leaves blown along the path scratched at the gravel with webbed fingers, like cut-off hands. I wanted to run away. When Danny was in the earth the gravediggers left. The parson and I sang a funeral hymn. The wind was roaring. As we were singing I heard another voice joining in in the distance. It was faint. I had been waiting for it. I didn't need to look round. I knew the sound of the voice and the clicking leg. They came closer and closer. Soon the voice was deafening, the sad hymn roaring like a waterfall beside me. Jordan came right up and stood between me and the parson, touching me. For shaking he was like a giant tree hurling off the storm. His little black book was in his hand. Even in the wind I could smell the strong mouldiness that came off him, clammy as grave-clay. He was bigger than ever. The brim of his black hat was spread out like a roof over my head. As he stood beside me he seemed to be absorbing me. He put his arm with the night-stick in his hand around my shoulders. I felt as though I was gradually disappearing inside his huge body. The ground all around me melted, the path began to flow faster and faster past my feet like a rushing river. I tried to shout out in my terror. I fainted.

When I came round the parson was beside me. We were sitting on the heap of earth beside Danny's open grave. I was as wet as the bed of the river with fright. When I spoke to the parson about Jordan he humoured me. That was a fortnight ago. Yesterday when I cut myself shaving I didn't bleed. All that came out of the cut was a drop or two of yellow water. I won't be long now. I am finished. I wouldn't advise anybody to try crossing Jordan.

OLD BEN

If you take the mountain road south from Hay over the Black Mountains, you will come to Llanthoney Valley, and it was here in the twelfth century the monks built their Priory. A mile or so below the Priory, David Hughes had his farm, *Coed Mynach* (The Monk's Wood). When of an evening the farmer took a walk up the road to the inn, his old sheepdog Ben would follow, literally in his master's footsteps, until they came to the gate which led to the winding lane that served as 'main road' for the valley. Then Ben would suddenly bound along the side of the hedge and disappear through his special exit, waiting at the roadside for his master to catch up with him. He never used the gate.

One morning Mrs Hughes found Ben lying in his *cwch* unable to stand. His glazed eyes and feebly wagging tail told her the end was near. That evening poor old Ben was dead.

A few days later Mr Hughes was preparing to take some sheep to the Market at Abergavenny. It was a good eight mile trek, even taking the side tracks. 'I won't take Frisk and Cumro,' he said, then sighed, 'I'll miss old Ben, and no mistake.'

That night he caught the bus that dropped him off at the Old Skerrid Inn and set off up the valley. He had not walked far when he heard the sound of a stone hitting tarmac, and swung quickly round; there was no mistaking two figures striding purposefully after him. There was no doubt in his mind that they were two 'yobos' he had seen lounging against the wall when he got off the bus. He had not paid much attention to them, but they must have recognised him for a farmer on his way home from market, and realised he would have a considerable sum of money on him.

He looked around for a thick stick with which to defend himself, but he could not find one, so he turned to face them, leaning against the bank so that he could kick out with his heavy farm boots. They were within a hundred yards of him, when out of the hedge sprang a dog. It stood in the roadway, fangs bared, growling low. The youths hesitated as the dog crouched to spring, then, thinking better of it, they turned and slunk off back down the road.

The farmer was still shaking, and for some reason he hardly dared look at the dog. He was fully aware that the animal was walking behind him, but he did not once look down. He was safe now, but his heart continued to thump, and he seemed to have lost all sense of time and distance. As he passed the spot old Ben used as his entrance, he became aware that the dog had left him. He turned then and looked – he was alone once more.

'Good heavens, Dai!' said his wife when he entered the farmhouse kitchen, 'you look as if you've seen a ghost.'

Her husband glanced towards the hearth rug where the two dogs lay basking in the warmth from the fire.

'Perhaps I have,' he said.

Hazel F. Looker.

A CRY OF CHILDREN

JOHN CHRISTOPHER

Bryncapil did not appear in the school atlas that I borrowed from my landlady, but I found it in the Oxford atlas in the local public library. It was sited on the outer slopes of the Flintshire hills, some miles north-west of Wrexham. This was not a part of the country I knew – I had only been to Wales once, as a child – but it looked attractive. There were plenty of jobs as locum going, but they all seemed to be in large cities. What I really wanted, after five years in the wartime Army followed by the years of medical grind, was a long rest among the Swiss Alps. Since I could not afford that,

Bryncapil seemed to offer a tolerable substitute. I wrote at once to Dr Merrick, and said I would be with him on the evening of the 15th. He wanted to leave on the 20th, and would be away six weeks.

The illusion I had built up, of a pretty little Welsh stone village, was nothing like the reality. Merrick met me at Wrexham and drove me up in a battered Morris saloon that had been far from new at the outbreak of war. We were soon off the main road, and the going rapidly worsened. The country was dull in sombre summer evening light, the hills dark and unpromising. It took us longer than I would have expected to reach our destination, which proved to be a mid-nineteenth century mining village, built in grimy red brick – a few straggling lines of terraced houses, three shops, the chapel, and a solitary pub, clinging to the hillside below the bleak black cones of slag-heaps and a broken-down mine working.

The mine, Merrick explained, had closed at the end of the war; he thought the owners had only kept it going till then in the hope of qualifying for compensation under nationalisation. Miners still lived there, and were taken by bus to the nearest pit, ten miles away. But that pit, too, was on the danger list. The village was dying, and fast. In one terrace of fifteen dwellings, only two were occupied. The shops only carried on because their owners were too old to start afresh. The pub was a brewery house, and there was talk that the brewery would be closing it down next winter.

After this, Merrick's own house was something of a surprise. It stood above and beyond the village, a large double-fronted place, not pretty but impressive, standing in grounds of upwards of an acre, with its own gateposts and drive. The gates themselves, though, had gone – taken for salvage during the war, he told me – and the drive was full of potholes which made the car's springs groan in protest. The door and windows had not been painted for years, and the hall smelt of damp and rot. Carpets were worn, curtains faded, the furniture shabby. The room to which he showed me was big and high-ceilinged, and the few bits and pieces – an iron bed, washstand, two upright chairs, oak-stained bookcase with evil-smelling books – seemed lost in it. There was a fireplace, but it did not look as though it had had a fire in it during this century. Merrick made a perfunctory reference to this. Since it was July, he had not thought a fire would be necessary, but it was true the weather was cold for the time of year. If I wanted a fire laid . . . I said no, not realising at that stage that to have said yes would have meant either he or I doing it. His only servant was a daily help, well past middle age, who came in most days but left as soon as she had prepared supper.

Over a whisky he told me something about the practice. Before the First World War it had been relatively prosperous, taking in an extensive rural hinterland well dotted with prosperous mansions and farms. The inter-war years, though, had been bad both for farmers and the landed gentry. The second war had put paid to the latter, and while farming had done a little better this had not improved his position much. They preferred to call in medical aid from Mold or Wrexham. He mentioned this with an air of faint surprise, apparently unaware how very unhelpful in this respect the house, and his own appearance, were.

My first feeling for him had been one of mild dislike, coupled with contempt. He could never have been a prepossessing man physically and now, in his forties, was obviously running to seed. His suit was prewar, of a cloth better than the utility material which at that time was all that was available, but it had not been looked after. It was baggy, with no semblance of a crease in it anywhere, and there were grease-marks and cigarette burns in plenty. He was tall, but thin and dyspeptic-looking, and had a manner that contrived to be brusque and apologetic at the same time. He would, I thought, have run any practice into the ground, let alone one as inevitably doomed as this.

But that was not my worry. I was merely hired to look after things for six weeks, and I reflected that if the surroundings did not come up to expectations, the amount of work was not likely to, either. I could do with the rest.

He had told me that our supper was on the top of the huge solid-fuel cooker in the kitchen, left there by Mrs Morgan, the daily help. I had only had a couple of sandwiches since breakfast, and was looking forward to a meal. He asked me if I would have another whisky, and I refused. He poured himself one, though, a very large one. It added a little more to the picture, which was becoming familiar. Our conversation, never sprightly, flagged badly. I stared at him in hungry and annoyed silence.

Things perked up a little when we finally got round to eating. The food was not inspiring, centring round a shepherd's pie, but I was young and had an appetite. Merrick merely toyed with his plate. As the edge of my hunger was taken off, I felt a little ashamed of my earlier muteness and tried to make conversation. It was Merrick's turn to be reticent. A fine prospect, I thought, for the four days in which we were to share this isolated and echoing building, like the man and woman in old-fashioned weather-houses, advancing and retreating, turn about.

But I drew him at least on the subject of some of the volumes in the bookcase in my room. I had seen several editions of Arthur Candover, and mentioned how the author had fascinated me as a child. He wrote stories of high romance, which I had loved. To my surprise, Merrick said:

'Me, too. He is a wonderful writer for children. I don't know anyone these days who understands the mind of a child as he does.'

'Is he still alive? I've not heard of him for some years.'

Merrick nodded. 'Alive. And not far from here. He has a house up in the hills, five or six miles away.'

'He's not a patient, though?'

'Not of this practice, nor any other. He and his wife lead very solitary lives. They scarcely ever leave the house, and they're anti-medical. They go in for nature cures, or something like that.'

'I'd like to meet him,' I said. 'Perhaps he'll get something nature can't cure.'

He looked at me aggressively. 'If nature can't, do you think you're likely to?'

'I think I would have a chance. Nature doesn't have the benefit of modern drugs.'

He stared at me, in a new silence. He had lost faith, I saw, in his profession, in his skills, above all in himself. I pitied and despised him.

There was, as I had thought, relatively little to do, and we saw a lot of each other during the days before his departure. We did not get on any better, and did not converse much. I got my own breakfast – Merrick did not eat any – and Mrs Morgan came in at nine and drifted, wraith-like, round the house until six. She was a poor cook, and a worse cleaner, but had the merit of unobtrusiveness. I was not finding the life too irksome – I had never been used to luxury – and was looking forward to the time when I would be on my own. Merrick, I noticed, started drinking at the end of six o'clock surgery (which could be a quarter past six for want of patients), and drank heavily both before and after supper, a combination which slightly shocked me. After the first evening, I refused the offers to join him even for one drink. Alcohol meant nothing to me, and I think I wanted to use my abstinence to underline his weakness.

On the last evening, though, with the prospect of taking him into Wrexham for the nine o'clock train next morning, I relented. We had endured a steak-and-kidney pie followed by gluey rice pudding, and I needed something to take the taste away. We had a whisky together, sitting in cracked leather arm-chairs in the large and once elegant drawing-room, and then another, and another. The little man and woman came out of the weather-house together: we were both ready to talk.

It was, to start with, a surprisingly co-operative effort. He asked me about my life and listened with attention and seeming interest, and I returned this. I learned for the first time that this was a family practice, started by his grandfather, passed to his father, and so to him. I learned that he had been married. His wife had died young, in childbirth, and the child had not survived.

Alcohol was not important to me, but that did not mean that it was without effect. He put more questions, and I talked more freely. Against his background, of a medical family with three generations training at the same teaching hospital, I set my own: starting from the working class, becoming a bank clerk, sights raised by being commissioned in the Army, taking advantage of a Government scheme to go to University and so on to medicine. I had carefully learned the ropes, played a fair game of Rugger, got on well with the right people . . .

'And the future?' he asked. 'What do you look for there?'

'Well, as you know, I'm going to Ambrose's as a houseman in the autumn.'

'Couldn't do better. And after that? Not general practice, I imagine?'

'I'm hoping to be able to specialise. ENT, possibly, or skins.'

'Both good choices,' Merrick said. 'Harley Street by the time you're forty. Skins are the better bet, I would think. Your patients never die, and none of them ever recover. You get a lot of rich women, too. You'll make a fortune.'

The sarcasm, though not stressed, was present. I said, trying to make it light:

'Better than the poorhouse.'

He paused and then, apparently, changed the subject. He had told me he was going to South Africa; now he explained that he had a sister out there, married to a farmer. She had been urging him to sell up and settle there, and this trip, which he could not really afford, was one of reconnaissance. He doubted if it would come to anything, though. He was not sure, really, that he wanted to uproot himself – in particular, to leave this house. It was not just a matter of having always lived in it. He had brought his wife here, and it was here she had died.

I thought how obvious were the rationalisations for failure. He knew he had no hope of making his way in a new and bustling country (South Africa had not then turned into a dirty word), and was justifying his defeat in advance.

He said: 'Her presence is with me, in this house. It might not be so somewhere else.'

I asked what he meant by presence. He said:

'Do you believe in survival?'

'After death? I'm afraid not.' I went on, mollifying: 'Memory keeps people alive, in a way.'

Merrick started to talk about his dead wife. He had been sure, at the beginning, that she was gone completely, that the spirit he loved had died with the stiffening body. This sense of loss and despair had lasted almost a year. Then, unexpectedly, he had become aware of her again – a sensation first, impalpable and fleeting; later something more real. He had heard her voice in the night, seen her once at the corner of the stairs.

I listened patiently as he talked. It was all part of the picture: a retreat from life that was not uncommon in isolated and weak characters. Another excuse for failure. I had not come across this particular illusion in a medical man before – one expected more scepticism from members of the profession – but the human mind, I knew, was capable of extremes of self-deception.

He seemed at last to become aware of my lack of response. He drained his glass and stood up.

'Bedtime, I think.' He paused, and looked at me. 'You're an admirable young man in many ways, Hobson. Personable, intelligent, determined. It's going to be a dull six weeks for you, tending this backwater.'

I shook my head. 'I don't think so.'

'But you can treat it as a very small detour on your road towards success. You have a great future ahead of you – I'm sure of that. You have all the positive qualities, and the one essential negative one: a lack of imagination.'

I could easily have matched his rudeness, but was not going to. I said stiffly:

'Well, thank you.'

'Nevertheless,' he said, 'a dull six weeks. Running a surgery in a decaying house, next to a dying village. I'm afraid I can't even offer you the hope of contact with the one thing you might find interesting, Candover has lived here twenty years without calling in a doctor, and I doubt if he will during the next six weeks. I'm sorry about that.'

A week later, driving the battered Morris along an unfamiliar minor road that wound round the side of a hill, I thought of Merrick's words. I was on my way to Candover's house. There are times when even the most resolutely anti-medical household must call the doctor in. Mrs Candover had telephoned me shortly after I had finished one of Mrs Morgan's dreadful suppers, or the little I could eat of it. Her husband had been stooping to tie a shoelace and had fallen. He was unconscious and breathing heavily. She had tried to bring him round without effect. She was plainly distressed, but managed to give me clear enough directions for getting to their home. I picked up my bag and left at once.

It was as well the directions had been clear, because they lived at the back of beyond. A cart-track led through wooded country for two or three miles, with no trace of man apart from a single telephone wire. Then, quite unexpectedly, the trees broke to reveal the house.

Dusk was thick by now. In the shade of the trees it had been almost night. The day lingered more here, and the lines of the house were clear. It stood beyond a rough meadow and a smaller immaculate lawn flanked by well-kept flower beds. It was long and low – one would call it a cottage, I supposed – but of striking elegance. The architecture belonged to the prosperous south rather than to these wild Celtic borders: there were two gable windows and square leaded panes. The slates were pantiles, in a warm red which sat well above the mellow honey-coloured stone of the walls. Everything was clean, fresh, well ordered. On a slightly smaller scale it might have been merely pretty. As it was, I thought it one of the most beautiful houses I had ever seen. A soft light gleamed behind some of the windows. I thought: when I am rich and successful, I will find myself a place something like this.

There was no doorbell, but a heavy knocker in well-polished brass, a dolphin with humped back and laughing eyes. Footsteps came almost at once, and the door was opened. A woman stood there. She said:

'I heard your motor. Thank you for coming so quickly, Doctor. But I am afraid you are too late.'

Her grief was evident, and immense, but she was dry-eyed. I judged her to be in her late forties. She had the kind of beauty that seems to come from a deep peace of mind, calm and fruitful. I thought of a forgotten school book, of Ceres, the Earth Mother. I said awkwardly:

'I'm so sorry. Are you sure . . .?'

'You'd better come in.'

I had time to notice that the house was as beautiful inside as out. In the hall, an oil-lamp hung from the ceiling, and Mrs Candover took another from an old polished oak table and led the way upstairs. The stairs creaked, but the creak was comfortable, in a way friendly. Candover lay on a Persian carpet beside his bed. She had wisely left him where he had fallen, merely putting a cushion under his head. But he was dead, all right: a classic coronary.

Usually death routs the actor who controls our bodies; there is no posing in a corpse, and no dignity. Candover was a rare exception. He lay as though asleep, a tall, well-figured man in his sixties, wearing evening dress trousers with a dark silk stripe, white immaculate shirt, and black tie. His hands, I saw, were beautifully kept, the nails manicured. His silvery hair had not been rumpled. I could not remember seeing a dead man look so distinguished.

I straightened up and said: 'I'm sorry. If I may use your telephone, I'll call the ambulance.'

'To take him away?'

'Well, yes . . .'

She shook her head. 'I would prefer not. Not so soon.'

'Of course. I merely thought that, being on your own . . .'

'If you could help me lift him on the bed.'

She showed tremendous competence. It was she who thought

of the need for boards, since rigor had not yet set in, and showed me where I could get some. She herself would undress and see to him, but she asked me if I would wait downstairs. There were drinks on the sideboard: she hoped I would help myself.

I poured myself a dry sherry out of a simple but exquisitely cut decanter, and studied my surroundings. I had not had much experience of tastefulness in interiors, but I could recognise the perfection here. The wood was mostly oak, very old, and with a patina of years, decades of careful polishing. The floor was of long high-grained wooden blocks, with four rugs, casually placed, that carried the unmistakable stamp of noble lineage. One cabinet was full of Sèvres, glowing green and gold in the light from the oil-lamp. A worked silver bowl, a foot across and almost as high, was filled with red and white roses.

It was exactly what one would expect of a home belonging to two people with money and leisure and a cultured appreciation of the good things in life. But there was something else. It was not, as such places usually are, irreconcilable with the thought of the children; on the contrary, it evoked them. I suppose the pictures on the walls had a lot to do with it: watercolours that were the originals of illustrations for Candover's books. Children, framed in strange worlds of romance, looked out of them, smiling. It was not merely that, though. So many of the smaller pieces had an aspect of what one could only call fun. A brass telescope, set near the window, which would entrance any boy. A model under glass of a South American hacienda, with minuscule cattle, tiny people sunning themselves, lilliputian cattle grazing. A shelf with dolls in exotic national dresses and, I discovered in a darker corner of the room, a doll's house – one of those large Victorian things, filled with miniature Victorian furniture, even to the diminutive antimacassars on the red velvet chairs. I had opened the front and was looking at this when Mrs Candover returned. Turning, I said:

'I hope you don't mind . . .'

'Of course not.'

'Have you had children?'

It was the awkward question of a callow young man, but she did not seem to mind it. She said:

'No. None, I'm afraid. But we like childish things.' Her face moved in a flicker of pain. 'We both liked them.'

I said: 'Can I pour you a drink?'

She nodded. 'Please. A sherry.'

We talked together, and I learned something of the life they had led. They had been, as Merrick had said, recluses. No servants: he had tended the garden and she had done her own housework. They preferred that to having people intrude on their private contentment. The telephone had been their only link with the outside world, and very little used. She cooked on an Aga – they were both fond of dishes casseroled for hours in the oven – and it also gave them as much hot water as they needed. They had no refrigerator, of course, but a good north-facing larder with stone slabs, and a stream at the back of the house which made an excellent wine-cooler. Her husband had been fond of white wines.

A doctor acquires a professional view of death very quickly. It is not, as it is for the layman, a sudden and shocking break in continuity, but something very close to the routine. I could ignore the man lying upstairs and, doing so, enjoy all this – the surroundings, the sherry, the company and conversation of this woman who remained, in her bereavement, lovely and gracious. My own mother had been a slattern.

But I realised I must not outstay my welcome. I made some tentative suggestion about leaving. She said:

'You have been very kind, Doctor.'

'No. I wish there had been something I could do.'

She hesitated. 'I am afraid it is too much to ask.'

'Please. If there is anything . . .'

'I feel suddenly that I do not want to be alone here to-night. It is probably silly. It is not that I am afraid of Arthur. That would be absurd. A sense of . . . well, loneliness.'

'I'll run you into a hotel, with pleasure.'

She shook her head. 'I could not leave him, either. I suppose – you could not stay the night? There is a guest room. But I imagine you will need to get back. Do forgive me.'

I thought of Merrick's big bare ramshackle house. I said:

'I'd be very glad to stay. Providing you do not go to any trouble over it.'

Her eyes rested on me. 'Thank you, Doctor. I am extremely grateful.'

We sat and talked for another couple of hours. I was a nervous young man in those days, bored and conscious of the slowness of time when I was not working. Here, in these surroundings, I felt entirely different. Mrs Candover impressed me more and more. There was no mistaking her grief and loss, but she covered it with serenity. Later, she prepared supper for me. I protested that I had already eaten, but she insisted, and it was true that my attempt on Mrs Morgan's unpleasant stew was by now an unhappy memory. A little cold collation, she said. There was pork pie she had made herself, roast chicken, sweet-cured ham, lettuce and tomatoes and minted new potatoes from the garden, and a mayonnaise the like of which I never found again. She would not eat anything herself except a buttered crust of bread, but she had a glass from the bottle of white Burgundy which she brought in from its nest in the stream. They always had wine with their evening meal, she explained, just as they always dressed for it. Arthur had been getting ready when . . .

Her eyes shut for a moment. It had been, plainly, a wonderful marriage and partnership, the bond between them augmented rather than diminished by the absence of the children they both longed for, and whose laughter almost seemed to echo from the next room.

When I had finished she cleared away, refusing my offer of help, and then excused herself. She felt tired. I knew my room. If there was anything I wanted . . .

It was a small room, with a gabled window and a low ceiling, simply furnished but, like the rest of the house, in perfect taste. My bed had been aired with an old-fashioned warming-pan. There was a feather mattress, feather pillows, crisp snowy sheets. On the walls were more illustrations from Candover's books, mostly pen-and-ink. The faces of children smiled at me. A bookcase by the side of the bed had copies of his books. I picked one up that I had read when I was seven or eight and, in the dim light of the oil-lamp, began reading it again.

More than the story, it was the warmth for his characters, his children, that came over. I thought of their shared desire, lifted and transmuted into this. It was not often that human inadequacy and loss bloomed so well. Drowsiness and the warmth and comfort of the bed overcame me. I fell asleep, and during the night I dreamed.

It was a strange dream, because it involved none of the usual dislocations in space and time. I was here, in this same room and bed, and the time was now. All that was added was the voices – voices of children, crying out. I could not make out how many there were, nor what they were saying, but I was conscious of great sadness. They needed help. I had never cared much for children, being too preoccupied with my own concerns, but their desolation reached me, and I wanted to go to them. But in the dream I could not move. I struggled against my unwilling limbs and, in the struggle, came awake. The lamp still burned, the room was as peaceful as before. And the voices, of course, had ceased.

I smoked a cigarette and lay awake, thinking. Was this the supernatural in which Merrick so firmly believed? But how different a manifestation, if so. Not the dead, but the unborn. The ones who should have filled this house, whose presence had been so lovingly prepared, whose absence was the one shadow on a life of grace and love.

I talked to Merrick about it after he had come back. I had no feeling of sympathy with him, but I wanted to talk to someone, and the following day I would be leaving Bryncapil and would see neither him nor it again. He listened, but, I thought, without much interest. It was not, after all, his kind of supernatural. And the trip to South Africa had not answered his hopes. Although he had not said so in so many words, it was clear that he had come back resigned to his decaying house and practice.

He asked: 'Did you see her again?'

'Mrs Candover? No. She moved out the following day, when the undertakers collected the body. I believe she stayed in a hotel until the funeral and then went to London.'

I did not mention that I had telephoned her at the hotel, asking if there was anything I could do to help, and that my offer had been pleasantly but very finally refused. It was clear that she did not want to take our acquaintance further. I recognised a rebuff, and in those days was ashamed of such things.

'Is the house up for sale?'

'No. It's standing empty – the furniture's gone – but I gather she doesn't intend to sell.'

I had gone to the trouble of inquiring of the chief estate agent in the district. There was still this wishful thought of owning such a place, some day. Apparently he had tactfully asked Mrs Candover and received a flat no. The house was not to be sold. He pointed out that, empty, it would deteriorate and lose value. It made no difference; she would not budge.

Merrick said reflectively: 'Strange people.'

And you, I thought – living out the fag-end of your life in this squalor and hopelessness: I suppose that's not strange? I said:

'I should like to have known him. She's a fine person.'

He looked at me. 'The episode' – he lingered over the word – 'seems to have had a powerful effect on you.' I did not answer. 'Another whisky?'

'No.' I shook my head. 'I think I'll be getting to bed.'

I was sorry I had not met Candover, sorry I was unlikely to meet his wife again; but I had no regrets about Merrick, in a few hours' time, passing out of my life for ever.

But it was not for ever. Our paths crossed once more, and in the improbable way that jolts the mind and sets one looking for purposes and meanings. This was seventeen years later, and in Lagos. I had come in for drugs which were badly needed at the Clinic, and which some fool had consigned by boat instead of air. I ran into Merrick in one of the main streets, hesitated, and halted as he recognised me. I imagine we had both changed a great deal, but I was shocked by the difference in him. He had aged tremendously, and his face was yellow. He said :

'Hobson! What an extraordinary coincidence. Come and have a drink with me.'

I hesitated for a moment. I had the drugs and wanted to get back with them. I did not particularly want to talk to Merrick. But it would have been rude to refuse, and I could not pretend that half an hour would make any tremendous difference. There was a bar in a hotel nearby which I sometimes used. We went there, and found ourselves the only whites in a noisy assembly of prosperous Negroes. He ordered whiskies for both of us, and started to talk.

He had come on the same ship as my drugs, putting in here on the way to Cape Town. Another visit to his sister, I suggested? He hesitated, and agreed.

'And another locum at Bryncapil?'

'No. I've retired.'

'Lucky man.'

'Not exactly. The fact is, they've given me six months. Give or take a couple – you know how it is.' He bared his teeth in a smile. 'Carcinoma of the liver.'

One can be glib and reassuring to laymen under some circumstances, but never to a fellow professional. I said :

'I'm very sorry.'

He nodded. 'Well, it comes to all of us, one way or another. And I'm lucky that it's one of the less painful varieties.' He grinned, his teeth very white against the yellow of his face. 'Tell me about yourself. Are you married?'

'Yes.'

'Children?'

'No. We can't have any, unfortunately.'

'And you're working out here?'

I told him briefly about the Clinic. We handled adults, but our chief concern was with the young. Yaws, famine fever, bilharzia, trypanosomiasis, leprosy . . . there was plenty to keep us busy. We were training African staff to take over eventually, but it would be some years before that could happen.

'So I was wrong,' Merrick said. 'It didn't turn out to be Harley Street after all.'

'No.'

He sat back, staring at me. 'Do you remember – we talked about the supernatural . . . and you told me about the dream you had in Candover's house?' I nodded. 'Did that affect your life, do you think?'

I hesitated, unwilling to disclose privacies to this man I scarcely knew and still disliked. I said:

'I don't know. Possibly.'

'And the outcome – that didn't shock you?'

'It's a country that takes some getting used to. There are difficulties, but there would be in any life. I believe I enjoy mine more than most.'

He said impatiently: 'You misunderstand me. I was referring to the Candover case.'

'I'm sorry. I don't know what you're talking about.'

'It was in all the papers . . . oh, eighteen months ago.'

'The English papers do get out here eventually, but I'm afraid I don't read them.'

So he told me. Of how, following Mrs Candover's death, her estate had passed to a distant nephew. It included the house, up above Bryncapil, which he sold. After lying empty all those years, it needed extensive repairs, to the roof particularly. Workmen had found them in a corner of the loft – four small bundles, each wrapped in a blanket.

I said: 'They could have been there when the Candovers took the house.'

'The pathologist was able to date them quite accurately. The blankets had helped to preserve them.'

'Then they could have been natural deaths. Reporting would have meant their life being invaded. They had a horror of that.'

'Four of them?' Merrick said. 'And in any case . . . they found a small feather in the lung of one.'

I thought of the soft enveloping feather pillows on which my head had rested that night long ago. Pressed down over a small face that had only just fought and won the struggle to draw breath.

I said: 'But why? Why?'

'As you said, they had a horror of having their life invaded. Children are invaders. Small barbarians, wrecking the arts and graces. They loved the idea of the child. The reality . . .'

'Four times?'

' "After the first death there is no other." Everything turns into habit, including murder.' He finished his drink and beckoned to a waiter. 'Including the process of dying.'

'I suppose so.'

'Your dream, that night you spent there . . . the voices of children, crying for help. Most interesting. I thought of writing it up for a journal I know that deals with that sort of thing, but at second-hand it wouldn't mean much. I suppose you wouldn't . . .?'

He shrugged. 'It would be subjective, anyway. They prefer more empirical stuff. And yet important in its effects. You wind up here.'

'Yes.'

'A cry for help,' Merrick said, 'but not the one you thought it was. Not the unborn, but the murdered innocents. Quite a difference.'

'No,' I said. 'Not really.'

THE CYOERAETH

There was a peculiar species of ghosts, denominated in Wales as *Cyoeraeth*, and deemed the most horrible of supernatural beings. The following is a description of it. A being with dishevelled hair, long black teeth, long lank withered arms; its shriek is described as having such an effect, as literally to freeze the blood in the veins of those who heard it, and was never uttered except when the ghost came to a cross road, or went by some water, which (if a female) she splashed with her hands, making at the same time the most doleful sounds, and exclaiming 'Oh! Oh *fy ngnr, fy ngnr*!' (my husband! my husband!) or (if a male) '*fy ngnraig*! *fy ngnraig*! (my wife! my wife!), or '*fy mlentyn, fy mlentyn, fy mlentyn bach*!' (my child, my child, my little child).

It is reported of a blacksmith residing at Trelech, Breconshire, that having occasion to work all night, he was disturbed about twelve o'clock by the dreadful shriek of the *cyoeraeth*, but supposing it to be 'some wilful person or persons' endeavouring to intimidate him, he imitated it, until it approached his shop, when it gave such a scream that almost terrified the poor blacksmith out of his wits, who instantly covered his fire with his apron, it being said that a ghost will not pass by a light; he related that a person whom he knew died soon after.

From *Cambrian Superstitions by W. Howells, 1831*

THE SHINING PYRAMID

ARTHUR MACHEN

'Haunted, you said?'

'Yes, haunted. Don't you remember, when I saw you three years ago, you told me about your place in the west with the ancient woods hanging all about it, and the wild, domed hills, and the ragged land? It has always remained a sort of enchanted picture in my mind as I sit at my desk and hear the traffic rattling in the street in the midst of whirling London. But when did you come up?'

'The fact is, Dyson, I have only just got out of the train. I drove to the station early this morning and caught the 10.45.'

'Well, I am very glad you looked in on me. How have you been getting on since we last met? There is no Mrs Vaughan, I suppose?'

'No,' said Vaughan, 'I am still a hermit, like yourself. I have done nothing but loaf about.'

Vaughan had lit his pipe and sat in the elbow chair, fidgeting and glancing about him in a somewhat dazed and restless manner. Dyson had wheeled round his chair when his visitor entered and sat with one arm fondly reclining on the desk of his bureau, and touching the litter of manuscript.

'And you are still engaged in the old task?' said Vaughan, pointing to the pile of papers and the teeming pigeon-holes.

'Yes, the vain pursuit of literature, as idle as alchemy, and as entrancing. But you have come to town for some time I suppose; what shall we do tonight?'

'Well, I rather wanted you to try a few days with me down in the west. It would do you a lot of good, I'm sure.'

'You are very kind, Vaughan, but London in September is hard to leave. Doré could not have designed anything more wonderful and mystic than Oxford Street as I saw it the other evening; the sunset flaming, the blue haze transmuting the plain street into a road "far in the spiritual city".'

'I should like you to come down though. You would enjoy roaming over our hills. Does this racket go on all day and all night? It quite bewilders me; I wonder how you can work through it. I am sure you would revel in the great peace of my old home among the woods.'

Vaughan lit his pipe again, and looked anxiously at Dyson to see if his inducements had had any effect, but the man of letters shook his head, smiling, and vowed in his heart a firm allegiance to the streets.

'You cannot tempt me,' he said.

'Well, you may be right. Perhaps, after all, I was wrong to speak of the peace of the country. There, when a tragedy does occur, it is like a stone thrown into a pond; the circle of disturbance keep on widening, and it seems as if the water would never be still again.'

'Have you ever any tragedies where you are?'

'I can hardly say that. But I was a good deal disturbed about a month ago by something that happened; it may or may not have been a tragedy in the usual sense of the word.'

'What was the occurrence?'

'Well, the fact is a girl disappeared in a way which seems highly mysterious. Her parents, people of the name of Trevor, are well-to-do farmers, and their eldest daughter Annie was a sort of village beauty; she was really remarkably handsome. One afternoon she thought she would go and see her aunt, a widow who farms her own land, and as the two houses are only about five or six miles apart, she started off, telling her parents she would take the short cut over the hills. She never got to her aunt's. She's still missing. That's putting it in a few words.'

'What an extraordinary thing! I suppose there are no disused mines, are there, on the hills? I don't think you quite run to anything so formidable as a precipice?'

'No; the path the girl must have taken had no pitfalls of

any description; it is just a track over wild, bare hillside, far, even, from a by-road. One may walk for miles without meeting a soul, but it is all perfectly safe.'

'And what do people say about it?'

'Oh, they talk nonsense – among themselves. You have no notion as to how superstitious cottagers are in out-of-the-way parts like mine. They are as bad as the Irish, every whit, and even more secretive.'

'But what do they say?'

'Oh, the poor girl is supposed to have "gone with the fairies", or to have been "taken by the fairies". Such stuff!' he went on, 'one would laugh if it were not for the real tragedy of the case.'

Dyson looked somewhat interested.

'Yes,' he said, ' "fairies" certainly strike a little curiously on the ear in these days. But what do the police say? I presume they do not accept the fairy-tale hypothesis?'

'No; but they seem quite at fault. What I am afraid of is that Annie Trevor must have fallen in with some scoundrels on her way. Castletown is a large seaport, you know, and some of the worst of the foreign sailors occasionally desert their ships and go on the tramp up and down the country. Not many years ago a Spanish sailor named Garcia murdered a whole family for the sake of plunder that was not worth sixpence. They are hardly human, some of these fellows, and I am dreadfully afraid the poor girl must have come to an awful end.'

'But no foreign sailor was seen by anyone about the country?'

'No; there is certainly that; and of course country people are quick to notice anyone whose appearance and dress are a little out of the common. Still it seems as if my theory were the only possible explanation.'

'There are no data to go upon,' said Dyson, thoughtfully. 'There was no question of a love affair, or anything of the kind, I suppose?'

'Oh, no, not a hint of such a thing. I am sure if Annie were alive she would have contrived to let her mother know of her safety.'

'No doubt, no doubt. Still it is barely possible that she is alive and yet unable to communicate with her friends. But all this must have disturbed you a good deal.'

'Yes, it did; I hate a mystery, and especially a mystery which is probably the veil of horror. But frankly, Dyson, I want to make a clean breast of it; I did not come here to tell you all this.'

'Of course not,' said Dyson, a little surprised at Vaughan's uneasy manner. 'You came to have a chat on more cheerful topics.'

'No, I did not. What I have been telling you about happened a month ago, but something which seems likely to affect me more personally has happened within the last few days, and to be quite plain, I came up to town with the idea that you might be able to help me. You recollect that curious case you spoke to me about at our last meeting; something about a spectacle-maker.'

'Oh, yes, I remember that. I know I was quite proud of my acumen at the time; even to this day the police have no idea why those peculiar yellow spectacles were wanted. But, Vaughan, you really look quite put out; I hope there is nothing serious?'

'No, I think I have been exaggerating, and I want you to reassure me. But what has happened is very odd.'

'And what has happened?'

'I am sure that you will laugh at me, but this is the story. You must know there is a path, a right of way, that goes through my land, and to be precise, close to the wall of the kitchen garden. It is not used by many people; a woodman now and again finds it useful, and five or six children who go to school in the village pass twice a day. Well, a few days ago I was taking a walk about the place before breakfast, and I happened to stop to fill my pipe just by the large doors in the garden wall. The wood, I must tell you, comes to within a few feet of the wall, and the track I spoke of runs right in the shadow of the trees. I thought the shelter from a brisk wind that was blowing rather pleasant, and I stood there smoking with my eyes on the ground. Then something caught my attention. Just under the wall, on the short grass, a number of small flints were arranged in a pattern; something like this:' and Mr Vaughan caught at a pencil and piece of paper, and dotted down a few strokes.

'You see,' he went on, 'there were, I should think, twelve little stones neatly arranged in lines, and spaced at equal distances as I have shewn it on the paper. They were pointed stones and the points were very carefully directed one way.'

'Yes,' said Dyson, without much interest, 'no doubt the children you have mentioned had been playing there on their way from school. Children, as you know, are very fond of making such devices with oyster shells or flints or flowers, or with whatever comes in their way.'

'So I thought; I just noticed these flints were arranged in a sort of pattern and then went on. But the next morning I was taking the same round, which, as a matter of fact, is habitual with me, and again I saw at the same spot a device in flints. This time it was really a curious pattern; something like the spokes of a wheel, all meeting at a common centre, and this centre formed by a device which looked like a bowl; all, you understand, done in flints.'

'You are right,' said Dyson, 'that seems odd enough. Still it is reasonable that your half a dozen school children are responsible for these fantasies in stone.'

'Well, I thought I would set the matter at rest. The children pass the gate every evening at half-past five, and I walked by at six, and found the device just as I had left it in the morning. The next day I was up and about at a quarter to seven, and I found the whole thing had been changed. There was a pyramid outlined in flints upon the grass. The children I saw going by an hour and a half later, and they ran past the spot without glancing to right or left. In the evening I watched them going home, and this morning when I got to the gate at six o'clock there was a thing like a half-moon waiting for me.'

'So then the series runs thus: firstly ordered lines, then the device of the spokes and the bowl, then the pyramid, and finally, this morning, the half-moon. That is the order, isn't it?'

'Yes; that is right. But do you know it has made me feel very uneasy? I suppose it seems absurd, but I can't help thinking that some kind of signalling is going on under my nose, and that sort of thing is disquieting.'

'But what have you to dread? You have no enemies?'

'No; but I have some very valuable old plate.'

'You are thinking of burglars then?' said Dyson, with an accent of considerable interest, 'but you must know your neighbours. Are there any suspicious characters about?'

'Not that I am aware of. But you remember what I told you of the sailors.'

'Can you trust your servants?'

'Oh, perfectly. The plate is preserved in a strong-room; the butler, an old family servant, alone knows where the key is kept. There is nothing wrong there. Still, everybody is aware that I have a lot of old silver, and all country folks are given to gossip. In that way information may have got abroad in very undesirable quarters.'

'Yes, but I confess there seems something a little unsatisfactory in the burglar theory. Who is signalling to whom? I cannot see my way to accepting such an explanation. What put the plate into your head in connection with these flint signs, or whatever one may call them?'

'It was the figure of the bowl,' said Vaughan. 'I happen to possess a very large and very valuable Charles II punch-bowl. The chasing is really exquisite, and the thing is worth a lot of money. The sign I described to you was exactly the same shape as my punch-bowl.'

'A queer coincidence certainly. But the other figures or devices: you have nothing shaped like a pyramid?'

'Ah, you will think that queerer. As it happens, this punch-bowl of mine, together with a set of rare old ladles, is kept in a mahogany chest of a pyramidal shape. The four sides slope upwards, the narrow towards the top.'

'I confess all this interests me a good deal,' said Dyson. 'Let us go on then. What about the other figures; how about the Army, as we may call the first sign, and the Crescent or Half-moon?'

'Ah, there is no reference that I can make out of these two. Still, you see I have some excuse for curiosity at all events. I should be very vexed to lose any of the old plate; nearly all the pieces have been in the family for generations. And I cannot get it out of my head that some scoundrels mean to rob me, and are communicating with one another every night.'

'Frankly,' said Dyson, 'I can make nothing of it; I am as much in the dark as yourself. Your theory seems certainly the only possible explanation, and yet the difficulties are immense.'

He leaned back in his chair, and the two men faced each other, frowning, and perplexed by so bizarre a problem.

'By the way,' said Dyson, after a long pause, 'what is your geological formation down there?'

Mr Vaughan looked up, a good deal surprised by the question.

'Old red sandstone and limestone, I believe,' he said. 'We are just beyond the coal measures, you know.'

'But surely there are no flints either in the sandstone or the limestone?'

'No, I never see any flints in the fields. I confess that did strike me as a little curious.'

'I should think so! It is very important. By the way, what size were the flints used in making these devices?'

'I happen to have brought one with me; I took it this morning.'

'From the Half-moon?'

'Exactly. Here it is.'

He handed over a small flint, tapering to a point, and about three inches in length.

Dyson's face blazed up with excitement as he took the thing from Vaughan.

'Certainly,' he said, after a moment's pause, 'you have some curious neighbours in your country. I hardly think they can harbour any designs on your punch-bowl. Do you know this is a flint arrow-head of vast antiquity, and not only that, but an arrow-head of a unique kind? I have seen specimens from all parts of the world, but there are features about this thing that are quite peculiar.'

He laid down his pipe, and took out a book from a drawer.

'We shall just have time to catch the 5.45 to Castletown, he said.'

II

Mr Dyson drew in a long breath of the air of the hills and felt all the enchantment of the scene about him. It was very early morning, and he stood on the terrace in the front of the house. Vaughan's ancestor had built on the lower slope of a great hill, in the shelter of a deep and ancient wood that gathered on three sides about the house, and on the fourth side, the south-west, the land fell gently away and sank to the valley, where a brook wound in and out in mystic esses, and the dark and gleaming alders tracked the stream's course to the eye. On the terrace in that sheltered place no wind blew, and far beyond the trees were still. Only one sound broke in upon the silence, and Dyson heard the noise of the brook singing far below, the song of clear and shining water rippling over the stones, whispering and murmuring as it sank to dark deep pools. Across the stream, just below the house, rose a grey stone bridge, vaulted and buttressed, a fragment of the Middle Ages, and then beyond the bridge the hills rose again, vast and rounded like bastions, covered here and there with dark woods and thickets of undergrowth, but the heights were all bare of trees, showing only grey turf and patches of bracken, touched here and there with the gold of fading fronds. Dyson looked to the north and south, and still he saw the wall of the hills, and the ancient woods, and the stream drawn in and out between them; all grey and dim with morning mist beneath a grey sky in a hushed and haunted air.

Mr Vaughan's voice broke in upon the silence.

'I thought you would be too tired to be about so early,' he said. 'I see you are admiring the view. It is very pretty, isn't it, though I suppose old Meyrick Vaughan didn't think much about the scenery when he built the house. A queer grey, old place, isn't it?'

'Yes, and how it fits into the surroundings; it seems of a piece with the grey hills and the grey bridge below.'

'I am afraid I have brought you down on false pretences, Dyson,' said Vaughan, as they began to walk up and down the terrace. 'I have been to the place, and there is not a sign of anything this morning.'

'Ah, indeed. Well, suppose we go round together.'

They walked across the lawn and went by a path through the ilex shrubbery to the back of the house. There Vaughan pointed out the track leading down to the valley and up to the heights above the wood, and presently they stood beneath the garden wall, by the door.

'Here, you see, it was,' said Vaughan, pointing to a spot on the turf. 'I was standing just where you are now that morning I first saw the flints.'

'Yes, quite so. That morning it was the Army, as I call it; then the Bowl, then the Pyramid, and, yesterday, the Half-moon. What a queer old stone that is,' he went on, pointing to a block of limestone rising out of the turf just beneath the wall. 'It looks like a sort of dwarf pillar, but I suppose it is natural.'

'Oh, yes, I think so. I imagine it was brought here, though, as we stand on the red sandstone. No doubt it was used as a foundation stone for some older building.'

'Very likely.' Dyson was peering about him attentively, looking from the ground to the wall, and from the wall to the deep wood that hung almost over the garden and made the place dark even in the morning.

'Look here,' said Dyson at length, 'it is certainly a case of children this time. Look at that.'

He was bending down and staring at the dull red surface

of the mellowed bricks of the wall. Vaughan came up and looked hard where Dyson's finger was pointing, and could scarcely distinguish a faint mark in deeper red.

'What is it?' he said. 'I can make nothing of it.'

'Look a little more closely. Don't you see it is an attempt to draw the human eye?'

'Ah, now I see what you mean. My sight is not very sharp. Yes, so it is, it is meant for an eye, no doubt, as you say. I thought the children learnt drawing at school.'

'Well, it is an odd eye enough. Do you notice the peculiar almond shape; almost like the eye of a Chinaman?'

Dyson looked meditatively at the work of the undeveloped artist, and scanned the wall again, going down on his knees in the minuteness of his inquisition.

'I should like very much,' he said at length, 'to know how a child in this out-of-the-way place could have any idea of the shape of the Mongolian eye. You see the average child has a very distinct impression of the subject; he draws a circle, or something like a circle, and puts a dot in the centre. I don't think any child imagines that the eye is really made like that; it's just a convention of infantile art. But this almond-shaped thing puzzles me extremely. Perhaps it may be derived from a gilt Chinaman on a tea-canister in the grocer's shop. Still that's hardly likely.'

'But why are you so sure it was done by a child?'

'Why! Look at the height. These old-fashioned bricks are little more than two inches thick; there are twenty courses from the ground to the sketch if we call it so; that gives a height of three and a half feet. Now, just imagine you are going to draw something on this wall. Exactly; your pencil, if you had one, would touch the wall somewhere on the level with your eyes, that is, more than five feet from the ground. It seems therefore, a very simple deduction to conclude that this eye on the wall was drawn by a child about ten years old.'

'Yes, I had not thought of that. Of course one of the children must have done it.'

'I suppose so; and yet as I said, there is something singularly unchildlike about those two lines, and the eyeball itself, you see, is almost an oval. To my mind, the thing has an odd, ancient air; and a touch that is not altogether pleasant. I cannot help fancying that if we could see a whole face from the same hand it would not be altogether agreeable. However, that is nonsense, after all, and we are not getting further in our investigations. It is odd that the flint series has come to such an abrupt end.'

The two men walked away towards the house, and as they went in at the porch there was a break in the grey sky, and a gleam of sunshine on the grey hill before them.

All the day Dyson prowled meditatively about the fields and woods surrounding the house. He was thoroughly and completely puzzled by the trivial circumstances he proposed to elucidate, and now he again took the flint arrow-head from his pocket, turning it over and examining it with deep attention. There was something about the thing that was altogether different from the specimens he had seen at the museums and private collections; the shape was of a distinct type, and around the edge there was a line of little punctured dots, apparently a suggestion of ornament. Who, thought Dyson, could possess such things in so remote a place; and who, possessing the flints, could have put them to the fantastic use of designing meaningless figures under Vaughan's garden wall? The rank absurdity of the whole affair offended him unutterably; and as one theory after another rose in his mind only to be rejected, he felt strongly tempted to take the next train back to town. He had seen the silver plate which Vaughan treasured, and had inspected the punch-bowl, the gem of the collection, with close attention; and what he saw and his interview with the butler convinced him that a plot to rob the strong-box was out of the limits of inquiry. The chest in which the bowl was kept, a heavy piece of mahogany, evidently dating from the beginning of the century, was certainly strongly suggestive of a pyramid, and Dyson was at first inclined to the inept manœuvres of the detective, but a little sober thought convinced him of the impossibility of the burglary hypothesis, and he cast wildly about for something more satisfying. He asked Vaughan if there were any gypsies in the neighbourhood, and heard that the Romany had not been seen for years. This dashed him a good deal, as he knew the gypsy habit of leaving queer hieroglyphics on the line of march, and had been much elated when the thought occurred to him. He was facing Vaughan by the old-fashioned hearth when he put the question, and leaned back in his chair in disgust at the destruction of his theory.

'It is odd,' said Vaughan, 'but the gypsies never trouble us here. Now and then the farmers find traces of fires in the wildest part of the hills, but nobody seems to know who the fire-lighters are.'

'Surely that looks like gypsies?'

'No, not in such places as those. Tinkers and gypsies and wanderers of all sorts stick to the roads and don't go very far from the farmhouses.'

'Well, I can make nothing of it. I saw the children going by this afternoon, and, as you say, they ran straight on. So we shall have no more eyes on the wall at all events.'

'No, I must waylay them one of these days and find out who is the artist.'

The next morning when Vaughan strolled in his usual course from the lawn to the back of the house he found Dyson already awaiting him by the garden door, and evidently in a state of high excitement, for he beckoned furiously with his hand, and gesticulated violently.

'What is it?' asked Vaughan. 'The flints again?'

'No; but look here, look at the wall. There; don't you see it?'

'There's another of those eyes!'

'Exactly. Drawn, you see, at a little distance from the first, almost on the same level, but slightly lower.'

'What on earth is one to make of it? It couldn't have been done by the children; it wasn't there last night, and they won't pass for another hour. What can it mean?'

'I think the very devil is at the bottom of all this,' said

Dyson. 'Of course, one cannot resist the conclusion that these infernal almond eyes are to be set down to the same agency as the devices in the arrow-heads; and where that conclusion is to lead us is more than I can tell. For my part, I have to put a strong check on my imagination, or it would run wild.'

'Vaughan,' he said, as they turned away from the wall, 'has it struck you that there is one point – a very curious point – in common between the figures done in flints and the eyes drawn on the wall?'

'What is that?' asked Vaughan, on whose face there had fallen a certain shadow of indefinite dread.

'It is this. We know that the signs of the Army, the Bowl, the Pyramid, and the Half-moon must have been done at night. Presumably they were meant to be seen at night. Well, precisely the same reasoning applies to those eyes on the wall.'

'I do not quite see your point.'

'Oh, surely. The nights are dark just now, and have been very cloudy. I know, since I came down. Moreover, those overhanging trees would throw that wall into deep shadow even on a clear night.'

'Well?'

'What struck me was this. What very peculiarly sharp eyesight they, whoever "they" are, must have to be able to arrange arrow-heads in intricate order in the blackest shadow of the wood, and then draw the eyes on the wall without a trace of bungling, or a false line.'

'I have read of persons confined in dungeons for many years who have been able to see quite well in the dark,' said Vaughan.

'Yes,' said Dyson, 'there was the abbé in *Monte Cristo*. But it is a singular point.'

III

'Who was that old man that touched his hat to you just now?' said Dyson, as they came to the bend of the lane near the house.

'Oh, that was old Trevor. He looks very broken, poor old fellow.'

'Who is Trevor?'

'Don't you remember? I told you the story that afternoon I came to your rooms – about a girl named Annie Trevor, who disappeared in the most inexplicable manner about five weeks ago. That was her father.'

'Yes, yes, I recollect now. To tell the truth I had forgotten all about it. And nothing has been heard of the girl?'

'Nothing whatever. The police are quite at fault.'

'I am afraid I did not pay very much attention to the details you gave me. Which way did the girl go?'

'Her path would take her right across those wild hills above the house; the nearest point in the track must be about two miles from here.'

'Is it near that little hamlet I saw yesterday?'

'You mean Croesyceiliog, where the children come from? No; it goes more to the north.'

'Ah, I have never been that way.'

They went into the house, and Dyson shut himself up in his room, sunk deep in doubtful thought, but yet with the shadow of a suspicion growing within him that for a while haunted his brain, all vague and fantastic, refusing to take definite form. He was sitting by the open window and looking out on the valley and saw, as if in a picture, the intricate winding of the brook, the grey bridge, and the vast hills rising beyond; all still and without a breath of wind to stir the mystic hanging woods, and the evening sunshine glowed warm on the bracken, and down below a faint mist, pure white, began to rise from the stream. Dyson sat by the window as the day darkened and the huge bastioned hills loomed vast and vague, and the woods became dim and more shadowy; and altogether impossible. He passed the rest of the evening in a reverie, hardly hearing what Vaughan said; and when he took his candle in the hall, he paused a moment before bidding his friend good night.

'I want a good rest,' he said. 'I have got some work to do to-morrow.'

'Some writing, you mean?'

'No. I am going to look for the Bowl.'

'The Bowl! If you mean my punch-bowl, that is safe in the chest.'

'I don't mean the punch-bowl. You may take my word for it that your plate has never been threatened. No; I will not bother you with any suppositions. We shall in all probability have something much stronger than suppositions before long. Good night, Vaughan.'

The next morning Dyson set off after breakfast. He took the path by the garden wall, and noted that there were now eight of the weird almond eyes dimly outlined on the brick.

'Six days more,' he said to himself, but as he thought over the theory he had formed, he shrank, in spite of strong conviction, from such a wildly incredible fancy. He struck up through the dense shadows of the wood, and at length came out on the bare hillside, and climbed higher and higher over the slippery turf, keeping well to the north, and following the indications given him by Vaughan. As he went on, he seemed to mount ever higher above the world of human life and customary things; to his right he looked at a fringe of orchard and saw a faint blue smoke rising like a pillar; there was the hamlet from which the children came to school, and there the only sign of life, for the woods embowered and concealed Vaughan's old grey house. As he reached what seemed the summit of the hill, he realised for the first time the desolate loneliness and strangeness of the land; there was nothing but grey sky and grey hill, a high, vast plain that seemed to stretch on for ever and ever, and a faint glimpse of a blue-peaked mountain far away and to the north. At length he came to the path, a slight track scarcely noticeable, and from its position and by what Vaughan had told him he knew that it was the way the lost girl, Annie Trevor, must have taken. He followed the path on the bare hill-top, noticing the great limestone rocks that cropped out of the turf, grim and hideous, and of an aspect as forbidding as an idol of the South Seas; and suddenly he halted astonished, although he had found what he searched for. Almost without warning the ground shelved suddenly away on all sides, and Dyson looked down into a circular depression, which might well have been a Roman amphitheatre, and the ugly crags of limestone rimmed it round as if with a broken wall. Dyson walked round the hollow, and noted the position of the stones, and then turned on his way home.

'This,' he thought to himself, 'is more than curious. The Bowl is discovered, but where is the Pyramid?'

'My dear Vaughan,' he said, when he got back, 'I may tell you that I have found the Bowl, and that is all I shall tell you for the present. We have six days of absolute inaction before us; there is really nothing to be done.'

IV

'I have just been round the garden,' said Vaughan one morning. 'I have been counting those infernal eyes, and I find there are fourteen of them. For heaven's sake, Dyson, tell me what the meaning of it all is.'

'I should be very sorry to attempt to do so. I may have guessed this or that, but I always make it a principle to keep my guesses to myself. Besides, it is really not worth while anticipating events; you will remember my telling you that we had six days of inaction before us? Well, this is the sixth day, and the last of idleness. Tonight I propose we take a stroll.'

'A stroll! Is that all the action you mean to take?'

'Well, it may show you some very curious things. To be plain, I want you to start with me at nine o'clock this evening for the hills. We may have to be out all night, so you had better wrap up well, and bring some of that brandy.'

'Is it a joke?' asked Vaughan, who was bewildered with strange events and strange surmises.

'No, I don't think there is much joke in it. Unless I am much mistaken we shall find a very serious explanation of the puzzle.

You will come with me, I am sure?'

'Very good. Which way do you want to go?'

'By the path you told me of; the path Annie Trevor is supposed to have taken.'

Vaughan looked white at the mention of the girl's name.

'I did not think you were on that track,' he said. 'I thought it was the affair of those devices in flint and of the eyes on the wall that you were engaged on. It's no good saying any more, but I will go with you.'

At a quarter to nine that evening the two men set out, taking the path through the wood, and up the hillside. It was a dark and heavy night, the sky was thick with clouds, and the valley full of mist, and all the way they seemed to walk in a world of shadow and gloom, hardly speaking, and afraid to break the haunted silence. They came out at last on the steep hillside, and instead of the oppression of the wood there was the long, dim sweep of the turf, and higher, the fantastic limestone rocks hinted horror through the darkness, and the wind sighed as it passed across the mountain to the sea, and in its passage beat chill about their hearts. They seemed to walk on and on for hours, and the dim outline of the hill still stretched before them, and the haggard rocks still loomed through the darkness, when suddenly Dyson whispered, drawing his breath quickly, and coming close to his companion.

'Here,' he said, 'we will lie down. I do not think there is anything yet.'

'I know the place,' said Vaughan, after a moment. 'I have often been by in the daytime. The country people are afraid to come here, I believe; it is supposed to be a fairies' castle, or something of the kind. But why on earth have we come here?'

'Speak a little lower,' said Dyson. 'It might not do us any good if we are overheard.'

'Overheard here! There is not a soul within three miles of us.'

'Possibly not; indeed, I should say certainly not. But there might be a body somewhat nearer.'

'I don't understand you in the least,' said Vaughan, whispering to humour Dyson, 'but why have we come here?'

'Well, you see this hollow before us is the Bowl. I think we had better not talk even in whispers.'

They lay full length upon the turf; the rock between their faces and the Bowl, and now and again, Dyson, slouching his dark, soft hat over his forehead, put out the glint of an eye, and in a moment drew back, not daring to take a prolonged view. Again he laid an ear to the ground and listened, and the hours went by, and the darkness seemed to blacken, and the faint sigh of the wind was the only sound.

Vaughan grew impatient with this heaviness of silence, this watching for indefinite terror; for to him there was no shape or form of apprehension, and he began to think the whole vigil a dreary farce.

'How much longer is this to last?' he whispered to Dyson, and Dyson who had been holding his breath in the agony of attention put his mouth to Vaughan's ear and said:

'Will you listen?' with pauses between each syllable, and in the voice with which the priest pronounces the awful words.

Vaughan caught the ground with his hands, and stretched forward, wondering what he was to hear. At first there was nothing, and then a low and gentle noise came very softly from the Bowl, a faint sound, almost indescribable, but as if one held the tongue against the roof of the mouth and expelled the breath. He listened eagerly and presently the noise grew louder, and became a strident and horrible hissing as if the pit beneath boiled with fervent heat, and Vaughan, unable to remain in suspense any longer, drew his cap half over his face in imitation of Dyson, and looked down to the hollow below.

It did, in truth, stir and seethe like an infernal cauldron. The whole of the sides and bottom tossed and writhed with vague and restless forms that passed to and fro without the sound of feet, and gathered thick here and there and seemed to speak to one another in those tones of horrible sibilance, like the hissing of snakes, that he had heard. It was as if the sweet turf and the cleanly earth had suddenly become quickened with some foul writhing growth. Vaughan could not draw back his face, though he felt Dyson's finger touch him, but he peered into the quaking mass and saw faintly that there were things like faces and human limbs, and yet he felt his inmost soul chill with the sure belief that no fellow soul or human thing stirred in all that tossing and hissing host. He looked aghast, choking back sobs of horror, and at length the loathsome forms gathered thickest about some vague object in the middle of the hollow and the hissing of their speech grew more venomous, and he saw in the uncertain light the abominable limbs, vague and yet too plainly seen, writhe and intertwine, and he thought he heard, very faint, a low human moan striking through the noise of speech that was not of man. At his heart something seemed to whisper ever 'the worm of corruption, the worm that dieth not,' and grotesquely the image was pictured to his imagination of a piece of putrid offal stirring through and through with bloated and horrible creeping things. The writhing of the dusky limbs continued, they seemed clustered round the dark form in the middle of the hollow, and the sweat dripped and poured off Vaughan's forehead, and fell cold on his hand beneath his face.

Then, it seemed done in an instant, the loathsome mass melted and fell away to the sides of the Bowl, and for a moment Vaughan saw in the middle of the hollow the tossing of human arms. But a spark gleamed beneath, a fire kindled, and as the voice of a woman cried out loud in a shrill scream of utter anguish and terror, a great pyramid of flame spired up like a bursting of a pent fountain, and threw a blaze of light upon the whole mountain. In that instant Vaughan saw the myriads beneath; the things made in the form of men but stunted like children hideously deformed, the faces with the almond eyes burning with evil and unspeakable lusts; the ghastly yellow of the mass of naked flesh; and then as if by magic the place was empty, while the fire roared and crackled, and the flames shone abroad.

'You have seen the Pyramid,' said Dyson in his ear, 'the

Pyramid of fire.'

V

'Then you recognise the thing?'

'Certainly. It is a brooch that Annie Trevor used to wear on Sundays; I remember the pattern. But where did you find it? You don't mean to say that you have discovered the girl?'

'My dear Vaughan, I wonder you have not guessed where I found the brooch. You have not forgotten last night already?'

'Dyson,' said the other, speaking very seriously, 'I have been turning it over in my mind this morning while you have been out. I have thought about what I saw, or perhaps I should say about what I thought I saw, and the only conclusion I can come to is this, that the thing won't bear recollection. As men live, I have lived soberly and honestly, in the fear of God, all my days, and all I can do is believe that I suffered from some monstrous delusion, from some phantasmagoria of the bewildered senses. You know we went home together in silence, not a word passed between us as to what I fancied I saw; had we not better agree to keep silent on the subject? When I took my walk in the peaceful morning sunshine, I thought all the earth seemed full of praise, and passing by that wall I noticed there were no more signs recorded, and I blotted out those that remained. The mystery is over, and we can live quietly again. I think some poison has been working for the last few weeks; I have trodden on the verge of madness, but I am sane now.'

Mr Vaughan had spoken earnestly, and bent forward in his chair and glanced at Dyson with something of entreaty.

'My dear Vaughan,' said the other, after a pause, 'what's the use of this? it is much too late to take that tone; we have gone too deep. Besides you know as well as I that there is no delusion in the case; I wish there were with all my heart. No, in justice to myself I must tell you the whole story, so far as I know it.'

'Very good,' said Vaughan with a sigh, 'if you must, you must.'

'Then,' said Dyson, 'we will begin with the end if you please. I found this brooch you have just identified in the place we have called the Bowl. There was a heap of grey ashes, as if a fire had been burning, indeed, the embers were still hot, and this brooch was lying on the ground, just outside the range of the flame. It must have dropped accidentally from the dress of the person who was wearing it. No, don't interrupt me; we can pass now to the beginning, as we have had the end. Let us go back to that day you came to see me in my rooms in London. So far as I can remember, soon after you came in you mentioned, in a somewhat casual manner, that an unfortunate and mysterious incident had occurred in your part of the country; a girl named Annie Trevor had gone to see a relative, and had disappeared. I confess freely that what you said did not greatly interest me; there are so many reasons which may make it extremely convenient for a man and more especially a woman to vanish from the circle of their relations and friends. I suppose, if we were to consult the police, one would find that in London somebody disappears mysteriously every other week, and the officers would no doubt shrug their shoulders, and tell you that by the law of averages it could not be otherwise. So I was very culpably careless to your story, and besides, there is another reason for my lack of interest; your tale was inexplicable. You could only suggest a blackguard sailor on the tramp, but I discarded the explanation immediately. For many reasons, but chiefly because the occasional criminal, the amateur in brutal crime, is always found out, especially if he selects the country as the scene of his operations. You will remember the case of that Garcia you mentioned; he strolled into a railway station the day after the murder, his trousers covered with blood, and the works of the Dutch clock, his loot, tied in a neat parcel. So rejecting this, your only suggestion, the whole tale became, as I say, inexplicable, and, therefore, profoundly uninteresting. Yes, *therefore,* it is a perfectly valid conclusion. Do *you* ever trouble your head about problems which you know to be insoluble? Did you ever bestow much thought on the old puzzle of Achilles and the Tortoise? Of course not, because you knew it was a hopeless quest, and so when you told me the story of a country girl who had disappeared I simply placed the whole thing down in the category of the insoluble, and thought no more about the matter. I was mistaken, so it has turned out; but if you remember, you immediately passed on to an affair which interested you more intensely, because personally. I need not go over the very singular narrative of the flint signs; at first I thought it all trivial, probably some children's game, and if not that a hoax of some sort; but your showing me the arrow-head awoke my acute interest. Here, I saw, there was something widely removed from the commonplace, and matter of real curiosity; and as soon as I came here I set to work to find the solution, repeating to myself again and again the signs you had described. First came the sign we have agreed to call the Army; a number of serried lines of flints, all pointing in the same way. Then the lines, like the spokes of a wheel, all converging towards the figure of a Bowl, then the triangle or Pyramid, and last of all the Half-moon. I confess that I exhausted conjecture in my efforts to unveil this mystery, and as you will understand it was a duplex or rather triplex problem. For I had not merely to ask myself: what do these figures mean? but also, who can possibly be responsible for the designing of them? And again, who can possibly possess such valuable things, and knowing their value thus throw them down by the wayside? This line of thought led me to suppose that the person or persons in question did not know the value of unique flint arrow-heads, and yet this did not lead me far, for a well-educated man might easily be ignorant on such a subject. Then came the complication of the eye on the wall, and you remember that we could not avoid the conclusion that in the two cases the same agency was at work. The peculiar position of these eyes on the wall made me inquire if there was such a thing as a dwarf anywhere in the neighbourhood, but I found that there was not, and I knew that the children who pass by every day had nothing to do with the matter. Yet I felt convinced that whoever drew the eyes must be from three and a half to four feet high, since, as I pointed out at the time, anyone who draws on a perpendicular surface chooses by instinct a spot about level with his face. Then again, there was the question of the peculiar shape of the eyes; that marked Mongolian character of which the English countryman could have no conception, and for a final cause of confusion the obvious fact that the designer or designers must be able practically to see in the dark. As you remarked, a man who has been confined for many years in an extremely dark cell or dungeon might acquire that power; but since the day of Edmond Dantés, where would such a prison be found in Europe? A sailor, who had been immured for a considerable period in some horrible Chinese *oubliette*, seemed the individual I was in search of, and though it looked improbable, it was not absolutely impossible that a sailor or, let us say, a man employed on shipboard, should be a dwarf. But how to account for my imaginary sailor being in possession of pre-historic arrow-heads? And the possession granted, what was the meaning and object of these mysterious signs of flint, and the almond-shaped eyes? Your theory of a contemplated burglary I saw, nearly from the first, to be quite untenable, and I confess I was utterly at a loss for a working hypothesis. It was a mere accident which put me on the track; we passed poor old Trevor, and your mention of his name and of the disappearance of his daughter, recalled the story which I had forgotten, or which remained unheeded. Here, then, I said to myself, is another problem, uninteresting, it is true, by itself; but what if it prove to be in relation with all these enigmas which torture me? I shut myself in my room, and endeavoured to dismiss all prejudice from my mind, and I went over everything *de novo*, assuming for theory's sake that the disappearance of Annie Trevor had some connection with the flint signs and the eyes on the wall. This assumption did not lead me very far, and I was on the point of giving the whole problem up in despair, when a possible significance of the Bowl struck me. As you know there is a 'Devil's Punch-bowl!' in Surrey, and I saw that the symbol might refer to some feature in the country. Putting the two extremes together, I determined to look for the Bowl near the path which the lost girl had taken, and you know how I found it. I interpreted the sign by what I knew, and read the first, the Army, thus: 'there is to be a gathering or assembly at the Bowl in a fortnight (that is the Half-moon) to see the Pyramid, or to build the Pyramid.' The eyes, drawn one by one, day by day, evidently checked off the days, and I knew that there would be fourteen and no more. Thus far the way seemed pretty plain; I would not trouble myself to inquire as to the nature of the assembly, or as to who was to assemble in the loneliest and most dreaded place among these lonely hills. In Ireland or China or the west of America the question would have been easily answered; a muster of the disaffected, the meeting of a secret society, Vigilantes summoned to report: the thing would be simplicity itself; but in this quiet corner of England, inhabited by quiet folk, no such suppositions were possible for a moment. But I knew that I should have an opportunity of seeing and watching the assembly, and I did not care to perplex myself with hopeless research; and in place of reasoning a wild fancy entered into judgment; I remembered what people had said about Annie Trevor's disappearance that she had been "taken by the fairies" I tell you, Vaughan, I am a sane man as you are, my brain is not, I trust, mere vacant space to let to any wild improbability, and I tried my best to thrust the fantasy away. And the hint came of the old name of fairies, "the little people", and the very probable belief that they represent a tradition of the prehistoric Turanian inhabitants of the country, who were cave dwellers: and then I realized with a shock that I was looking for a being under four feet in height, accustomed to live in darkness, possessing stone instruments, and familiar with the Mongolian cast of features! I say this, Vaughan, that I should be ashamed to hint at such visionary stuff to you, if it were not for that which you saw with your very eyes last night, and I say that I might doubt the evidence of my senses, if they were not confirmed by yours. But you and I cannot look each other in the face and pretend delusion; as you lay on the turf beside me I felt your flesh shrink and quiver, and I saw your eyes in the light of the flame. And so I tell you without any shame what was in my mind last night as we went through the wood and climbed the hill, and lay hidden beneath the rock.

'There was one thing that should have been most evident that puzzled me to the very last. I told you how I read the sign of the Pyramid; the assembly was to see a pyramid, and the true meaning of the symbol escaped me to the last moment. The old derivation from πυρ, fire, though false, should have set me on the track, but it never occurred to me.

'I think I need say very little more. You know we were quite helpless, even if we had foreseen what was to come. Ah, the particular place where these signs were displayed? Yes, that is a curious question. But this house, is, so far as I can judge, in a pretty central situation amongst the hills; and possibly, who can say yes or no, that queer, old limestone pillar by your garden wall was a place of meeting before the Celt set foot in Britain. But there is one thing I must add: I don't regret our inability to rescue the wretched girl. You saw the appearance of those things that gathered thick and writhed in the Bowl; you may be sure that what lay bound in the midst of them was no longer fit for earth.'

'So?' said Vaughan.

'So she passed in the Pyramid of Fire,' said Dyson, 'and they passed again to the underworld, to the places beneath the hills.'

THE BROWN HOBGOBLIN OF BEDD GELERT

The Brown Hobgoblin – This was one of the day-goblins, and generally appeared to lonely wayfarers when crossing from one district to another over mountain tracks. He would appear in the form of a rustic, clad in homespun and corduroy, wearing nothing on his head, and carrying a long stick like that of a shepherd. He invariably walked in front of the traveller, with his back towards him, but not on the ordinary path. He would keep alongside of the path, and would thus gradually draw his follower out of the way. After he had drawn the wayfarer far enough from the path, he would suddenly disappear behind some wall or heap, leaving his dupe in great perplexity and utter ignorance of his whereabouts.

This goblin would sometimes descend from the mountains into the glens and valleys, and would strut along the walls in the fields, and along the roadside; he would now and again pop his head over the hedges to look into the roads. Thus parents frequently warned their children not to loiter on their errands for fear that 'Bwbach Llwyd' would see them.

From *Bedd Gelert, Its Facts, Fairies, and Folk-Lore*, by D. E. Jenkins

ANIMALS OR HUMAN BEINGS

ANGUS WILSON

Fräulein Partenkirchen was a reserved girl. At twenty-seven she was still unmarried, and her quiet blonde prettiness was fading; her skin had a sallow look, her hair if not constantly cared for quickly became dry and scurfy, about her heavy eyelids there hung a mauve, translucent look. She was not very strong. The feeling that she had been left on the shelf preoccupied her and made her unresponsive in company. The many changes in the German political scene in her youth and the experiences of heavy air-raids had somehow startled her into permanent stillness. She never knew what to expect of people and so she never committed herself to expressing opinions.

It had cost her family a determined and united effort to make her accept the post of housekeeper to Miss Ingelow in Wales. To her, they pretended that the acquisition of fluency in English would help her to get a higher post in the secretarial world. Among themselves, they agreed that this was highly unlikely, but they asserted that in England she might perhaps find a husband. An easily adaptable, acquisitive, noisy, small shop-keeping family, they found her presence an irksome restraint, and they sent her to England because they wanted to be rid of her.

Since Miss Ingelow lived in the remote fastnesses of the Welsh Marches, Fräulein Partenkirchen was to be met at Liverpool Street by another English lady, a friend of Miss Ingelow's, Mrs Gosport, who was to put her on the train for the little town of Montgomery. Mrs Gosport was a big, motherly woman whose figure seemed to be coming to pieces. Childless, she had devoted her life to girls' clubs. She was pleasantly impressed by Fräulein Partenkirchen's neat appearance, nothing vulgar yet not dowdy, and with just enough lipstick to make one feel that she was a nice human girl. Mrs Gosport hoped that she was not too delicate for the post, but attributed her faded appearance to the long journey.

They had breakfast together at the Great Western Hotel before Fräulein Partenkirchen left for Wales. 'I don't know how you'll find Alice Ingelow. I haven't seen her for over three years. Of course, she's quite a character,' said Mrs Gosport, 'but she's a wonderful woman. She's given her life for others. In the last years before she retired to Wales, I'm afraid we drifted apart a bit. I can't really feel as strongly about animals as about human beings, can you?' Mrs Gosport's large, cow-like eyes appealed to Fräulein Partenkirchen, but if the German girl had any preference in the matter she did not express it. 'Well, perhaps you don't agree with me,' said Mrs Gosport, 'but it seemed such a waste when Alice Ingelow, who had done such wonderful work for girls and women, became entirely absorbed with animals. She was the first, you know, to get the canteens going for women munition workers in the '14 war. And so wonderfully human and cheerful. And then the last time I went to see her in a big house outside London, the place was filled with cats and dogs. I felt it terribly. It was vivisection that did it, of course. She became quite crazy about the subject. Well, of course, I *don't* care for the idea. I can't believe they couldn't make just the same discoveries without cruelty to animals, but all the same when there's so much *human* material in need of help. . . . But there you are, dear, I don't want to say too much. Alice Ingelow is a wonderful woman, one of our pioneers, but I did just want to warn you. Because if you didn't like animals, it wouldn't be a very happy post for you. You see, she's a very old lady and she's always been used to having her own way.' Once again Fräulein Partenkirchen did not say whether she liked animals or not, she only said that she would like another cup of tea.

When Fräulein Partenkirchen arrived at Montgomery station, there was no one to meet her, but she seemed to make little of the half-hour walk that lay in front of her to reach Miss Ingelow's house in the hills. The little town square was unusually crowded that evening, and people were standing in the columned doorways of the square red brick houses enjoying the last gleams of the September sunshine. Fräulein Partenkirchen's neat figure and the heavy suitcase she was carrying attracted quite a lot of attention, but she went on her way without appearing to notice anyone. The little drive that led up to Miss Ingelow's house was quite a steep ascent, and the girl paused once or twice to lay down her heavy load. The house itself was a rather elegant long white-stuccoed house of about 1840, with a veranda. The stucco, however, was peeling everywhere and the garden was a tangle of overgrown nettles and convolvulus among which a few hardy Michaelmas daisies and montbretia alone survived. Everything was dead and dusty. Except for Miss Ingelow, who came out to meet her. It was true that she was a very old lady, but she was also a very bright birdlike one. Despite the mannish crop and the heavy tweed skirt and coat, her old, wrinkled weatherbeaten face was so small and well-rounded and her blue eyes were so alive and twinkling that she seemed intensely feminine, like a little wrinkled kitten that had got wrapped in a heavy rug by mistake. Her voice, too, when it came was not the deep bark that one would have expected, but a light, intensely cultured, almost over-modulated noise like an actress trained in the old school.

She was at once brisk and cheerful and kind, and yet remote and dreamy. She took quick and entire charge of her new housekeeper, giving her tea and cosseting her after the long journey, and yet not explaining why she had done nothing to provide her with transport. 'Now *I* shall make the supper this evening,' she said, 'and then tomorrow you can take over. I'm getting very old, you see, and I don't want to do much but potter in the garden and look after the animals. I hope you won't get too bored with an old woman. There's nobody else, you know, but you and me.' 'But the animals?' asked Fräulein Partenkirchen, looking around the neat little dining-room with its refectory table and its horse brasses.

'Well, I've only got the two now, you know. Rufus and Maria. Or I *did* have, but Maria's just got a lot of little babies. so I'm afraid we're going to be rather a large family party.'

Fräulein Partenkirchen gave a wan smile. 'But where are they?' she asked.

'Oh! I have to keep them in upstairs. They will go after the little birds and we can't have that, can we?' Miss Ingelow said. 'At the moment Rufus has to be in his little house all by himself, he's jealous of his own children. Naughty Rufus! Come and see them,' she said, springing up most agilely from her pseudo-Jacobean chair. As they mounted the stairs, Miss Ingelow looked back at Fräulein Partenkirchen with rather a worried smile. 'I do hope you *like* animals,' she said 'Some foreigners aren't very fond of them, I think.'

Fräulein Partenkirchen did not reply.

'Well,' Miss Ingelow cried, throwing open the door of her bedroom, 'there's Rufus. Isn't he fine?'

Fräulein Partenkirchen did not reply to this question, she only said, 'He is very big.'

'Yes,' said Miss Ingelow. 'Have you ever seen a more beautiful coat or a finer tail? We're talking about you, Rufus, but you mustn't listen or you'll get conceited. He knows every word we say and he's got a bit of a swollen head already. And now we must say how do you do to Maria. There she is, a picture of mother love. Thirsty little things, aren't they? Poor Maria! But she doesn't mind, she knows it's Nature's way.'

'The big one is quite angry, I think,' said Fräulein Partenkirchen.

'Yes,' said Miss Ingelow. 'Wicked Rufus! He's so jealous! He bit me the other day. Yes, you, Rufus! Look at his magnificent whiskers. I call him Rufus because of the red colour of his lovely fur.' She jangled the little bell on Rufus's house. 'Yes, I know. Dinner time,' she said. 'They always know and they eat such a lot of meat, but that's better than the little birds. Auntie will go and get dinner,' she said to her pets.

'And to think,' she told Fräulein Partenkirchen, as they descended the stairs, 'I only just saved them from those wicked vivisectionists. The dustman was going to sell them to the hospital.' They went into the little drawing-room where all Miss Ingelow's little treasures were – her Crown Derby service and her Chinese ivory chess set and her two ostrich eggs. With its striped wallpaper and its bright chintzes it seemed quite homely and cheerful. A fire was burning in the grate. 'The evenings get so chilly now,' said Miss Ingelow. 'Now you sit and rest and I'll get their dinner. And then we can have our supper in peace.'

After Miss Ingelow had gone out of the room, Fräulein Partenkirchen waited a moment, then she crossed the hall and went into the dining-room. She opened her suitcase and took out a pad of writing-paper. She tore off one sheet and in pencil she wrote on it, 'I am going away again. I do not like animals.' She seemed more cheerful now that she had expressed her opinion. Then, picking up her suitcase, she walked out of the house. As she passed along the path through the high, waving Michaelmas daisies and the grubby montbretia, she heard Miss Ingelow go upstairs. Then as she reached the dusty beech hedge and the little gate, she heard one after another two loud shrieks. She was not surprised and she went on her way. There was no-one in the little town square to watch her leave. At the station she was told that she would have to wait an hour for the return train, but she sat quite reserved and silent in the waiting-room.

It was as well that she had not returned to the house, for she had seen quite enough that was horrible in the air-raids on Hamburg as a young girl. Upstairs, Miss Ingelow lay on the floor with her throat torn open. An enormous buck rat was hissing and scratching at the wires of a cage. It wanted to get to its doe and devour the young ones. Soon it would have eaten all the raw meat that Miss Ingelow had brought with her; and as she had closed the door of the room behind her, there would be nothing then for Rufus to devour except Miss Ingelow herself. But the little bells she had put on his cage jangled merrily.

Fräulein Partenkirchen's family were not at all pleased to see her back again. If anything, she seemed more reserved and her skin more sallow. As to this story of hers, it promised ill for her chances of marrying. Such hallucinations were the mark of hysterical old maids, not of desirable brides. Of course, there was always the chance that she had seen ghosts. A certain amount of sixth sense could be very attractive in a woman. It was an echt Deutsch quality uniting her with all the old Legenden and Märchen. But hardly if all she could see was ghost rats! Now if only she had said the old Englishwoman had been carried off by the Niebelungen or lured to her death by the Lorelei. As it was, it was all very disappointing.

THE MAN ON A BIKE

The village of Aberhowy is situated in the foot hills where the central mountain block slopes down towards Cardigan Bay. From the coast road, the way to the village runs up the valley for about four miles, and then over a spur to drop down again into Aberhowy. It is a narrow road with barely room for two cars to pass, and sometimes the mists are so dense that no motorist can see the white posts that have been placed near the drop.

David Bowen and his wife had lived all their lives in Aberhowy, and they were very proud of their son Gwynfor who was preparing to enter the Baptist Ministry. The time came when he was to be ordained, and they were looking forward to attending the ordination ceremony. Gwynfor wrote saying a friend had brought a car, and if it was all right with them, they would both come up, stay the night, and then take them back to Cardiff for the ordination.

Mr and Mrs Bowen were very excited. They had never owned a car – all David Bowen had was an old bike, so the prospect of driving all the way 'in style' with their son to Cardiff was something to be talked over again and again, and half the village heard about it in no time.

The journey never took place. The car carrying Gwynfor Bowen and his friend crashed through the white posts and burst into flames on the rocks below. Both occupants were killed. Eighteen months after Gwynfor's death, David Bowen passed away, and his wife sold up and went to live with her sister over in Brecon.

Twenty years later, in 1956, a Birmingham businessman and his wife came to live in Aberhowy. They had one daughter who was training to be a doctor, and they thought the world of her. She had not seen their new bungalow, but telephoned her mother to say she would motor down the following Wednesday. She said they were to expect her around four o'clock, but when six-thirty had struck her parents became very worried.

'I hope she gets here soon,' said her mother, peering out of the window. 'It's getting very foggy, and she doesn't know the road.'

At that moment they heard a car turn into the drive.

'There she is,' cried her mother, rushing to open the door; her daughter was just getting out of the car.

'Hallo, folks,' she called out, 'got here safe and sound.'

'How did you manage in this thick old fog?' asked her mother.

'Well,' said the girl, 'it was a bit dicey at first, no cats' eyes, and I thought once of leaving the car and walking, then I saw the rear light of a bicycle – an old man was riding it. So I kept behind him till I came to the first street lamp. But, do you know, I lost him then though he was just in front of me. Funny, isn't it?'

Their daughter was not the first one to be guided through the fog, as her parents were subsequently to learn.

Is David Bowen still trying to be of service to those who motor over the dangerous spur?

Hazel F. Looker

THE MORGAN TRUST

RICHARD BRIDGEMAN

Oddly enough, it was a small handbook entitled *Not the Highways* that set Selby Pyle on the track of the strange village in the mountains.

He bought the slim volume at the station kiosk because there happened to be a picture of Snowdon on the cover, and he had for some time been toying with the idea of spending a holiday in Wales.

He riffled idly through its pages, noting in passing that it had been written – not very well written – by one John Kilby; as he read, the train rattled him along the way to Guildford where there had been rumours of a cottage with strange noises.

For Selby Pyle, middle-aged gentleman of leisure and assured income, had an unusual hobby. He liked to call himself an 'Amateur Psychic Investigator.' And when his contemporaries asked, 'Why?' he would go into details, explaining that he used the word 'Amateur' to denote that he worked without payment, and not because he was lacking in knowledge or experience of his subject.

But if they asked, 'Why such a strange hobby?' he would become evasive. 'Because it's out of the ordinary,' was his usual lame excuse. Only in his more sanguine moments would he admit even to himself the real motive behind his pursuit.

And if they still persisted in their amazement that a portly and immaculately-clad gentleman with cherubic blue eyes, a shapeless blob of a nose which offered only the most precarious of resting-places for rimless spectacles, a soft baby-tight mouth and a series of flabby chins should adopt such a way of spending time and money, then Selby, squirming a little, and rubbing his thin flaxen hair with stubby white fingers would be driven to confess openly certain of his innermost secrets.

He would tell how, despite the fact he was a religious man, he had failed to find solace in the teachings of the Church, and that he had an overwhelming dread of being snuffed out like an ephemeral candle when his time came. He was searching, he would tell them, for proof positive of life in the hereafter.

He kept notes and pictures in voluminous folders. On the wall of his study was a large-scale map with the sites of past investigations marked with red dots. He had a supply of small blue flags which were to be used if ever his search proved fruitful. But although the map was a measle-rash of red spots, it was devoid of blue flags.

Every rumour that came to his ears he traced hopefully to its source. So when he read the few lines in his morning paper about the strange happenings at Guildford, he boarded the first train.

London melted away, fields and farms slipped by, and Selby flicked through his booklet, sighed a little and stopped just by chance at the page that contained the description of Cwmbach.

'This village,' Mr Kilby informed him through the medium of the pages, 'is one of the most isolated that I encountered. Situated in a hollow in the shadow of Crib Goch it is steeped in the past. There is an excellent hostelry – the "Bryn Mawr" – and I can heartily recommend it as a centre for the enthusiastic fisherman. The roads are in poor condition; the air is mild, being shielded from the northerly winds; the people are friendly, and there is a fund of local superstition and tales of hauntings to delight even the most hardened of travellers.'

Selby, himself a writer, wriggled a little at the rather formal and Borrowesque turn of phraseology. But all the same his interest quickened and his psychic nose quivered at the mention of 'tales of hauntings'. He took out his notebook, made a note of the author's name and discovered that the publisher of the booklet was a friend of his, who had published certain of his writings.

The Guildford investigation having proved, as he had feared, to be fruitless – a matter of faulty plumbing – Selby wasted no further time: he telephoned the publisher from a kiosk in the High Street. Armed with Mr Kilby's address he returned to London, dined and took a taxi to the home of John Kilby, M.A.

The author of *Not the Highways* was angular and elderly, had a domed forehead and watery eyes. He listened to Selby's request for further information about Cwmbach with a certain air of suspicion.

'I take it you are engaged on a similar work?' he commented heavily. Selby went to great pains to protest his innocence of such a thing, whereupon the other unbent enough to produce a file of notes which he explained had been the basis of the book in question.

'It must be three years since I wrote the book,' he offered. 'Cwmbach,' he toyed with the name. 'I remember a little. But so far as the – er – supernatural aspect is concerned, I know no more than I wrote. If I had,' he pointed out, 'then I should have put it in. After all, there is little enough one can write about a place of that size.

'Cwmbach,' he said thoughtfully to the ceiling. 'Grey stone cottages, a stream that runs down the main street and some grand views of the valley. But the name brings back something else . . . Now what was it?'

He sat for a while, staring at his notes; Selby waited with some impatience. So far as he was concerned, if Mr Kilby had nothing more to add about the hauntings, then the interview could well be terminated.

'Morgan,' Kilby said into the silence, ' – that was the name, Ifor Morgan. There was a picture of him in the pub, and when

I asked about it they told me the story.'

He stroked his chin, smiling a little. 'Not that it can be of any use to you; indeed, it was of no use to me. But interesting, from a psychological point of view, for all that. Ifor Morgan, it seemed, was something of a rascal in his day. Many years ago he set up a kind of a Trust Fund, getting most of the local people to subscribe to it. The idea being that he would build a new village for them; modern houses, you know, bring in power and water on tap. It was going to be built in a green valley, just below Cwmbach, and by all accounts it was going to be a proper Shangri-la.

'But of course, like all plans of that sort it fell flat. He did start the building, but without previous consultation with the local authority. In the course of time they came down on him like a ton of bricks. A stupid man more than a knave, perhaps; a visionary – a dreamer. There have been many such: their follies litter the countryside. But Morgan took it very badly . . .'

'I take it he is dead?' Selby asked with quickening interest.

'Good Lord, yes. This happened years ago. But the people of Cwmbach talk about it as if it were only yesterday. Three years ago, when I stayed at the "Bryn Mawr", there were still some alive who had actually subscribed to the fund, their life-savings had gone down the drain. But the strange thing about that – '

'Yes?' Selby encouraged.

'They seemed to bear no animosity. Rather, his memory had been kept alive with affection, almost reverence. Think of it; he'd done them out of thousands, for most of the village had subscribed, and all there is to show for it – and I went to see for myself – is a pathetic collection of grass-covered foundations and partly-built walls.

'There's no accounting for people,' he mused. 'They forget the money they lost, remembering only that he did try to make things better for them. They were very proud, jealously proud, of Ifor Morgan.'

Selby said: 'The tales of hauntings, you don't connect them with this unfinished village?'

'Llannef it was to be called,' Kilby told him. 'I made a note of the name, intending to look up its meaning – I have an interest in Welsh place-names. No, Mr Pyle, it was merely an idle word dropped by the landlord of the "Bryn Mawr" that led me to comment about it in my book. Now what was it he said?' He clicked his fingers. 'Of course. I asked if there were any local stories – the kind of thing I could put in my book, you know? He said that there are ghosts in any village worth its salt. Perhaps he was trying to be clever. Anyway, I enlarged upon it, and put it in for what it was worth.'

Selby left him then and returned to his own flat, wondering if it would be wasted effort if he were to journey to the mountains in search of the village. And it was only because he'd already decided to go to Wales anyway, that he made up his mind to include Cwmbach in his itinerary.

He went by car, starting off early the next morning, striking due north, and spending the night at Chester. The following morning saw him driving through the sunshine of the coast road, crossing the Conway bridge, and swinging through the coastal resorts. At Bangor he turned inland, his map taking him readily enough as far as Bethesda. From there onwards he found it more satisfactory to rely upon local directions and reached Cwmbach in time for lunch.

It was much as he had imagined. The mountains, brown and green with out-croppings of grey granite, almost encircled the village. Cwmbach was typically Welsh, with the small, low-roofed cottages clustered about the steep slate roof and tall chimneys of the inn. A bracken-brown stream bubbled merrily at one side of the main street.

White-aproned women and cloth-capped men smiled at him as he coasted past; children broke off their play to wave. Selby felt a pleasure in their welcome; the mountains behind came down like a curtain, cutting off the world of finance and worry, hydrogen bombs and guided missiles. He swung the car on to the cobbled forecourt of the 'Bryn Mawr'.

He went through an archway, and the landlord, stocky and chestnut-faced, bare-armed and wearing a blue waistcoat with gilt buttons, made quite a thing of shaking his hand.

The bar was a cheerful place, low-timbered and aglow with polished jugs and tankards. A heavy-framed picture on one wall dominated the room, and Selby went to look at it.

It was the portrait of Ifor Morgan of which Kilby had spoken; for the name was written below in a flowing old-fashioned script. The landlord came by his side, asking in a soft lilt if 'The gentleman would be staying overnight, or perhaps for longer?'

'A day or two,' Selby told him; then, tapping the picture, 'A fine-looking man.'

'Our Mr Morgan?' The voice was even softer, and there was certainly reverence. 'Indeed, a very fine man.'

And as Selby turned to look at the landlord, a phrase came to his mind, brought there by the expression on the brown, wrinkled face, 'I will lift up mine eyes . . .'

Ifor Morgan had the face of a patriarch, a deep-eyed, wide-set face that might have come from the Old Testament. He had the eyes of a dreamer, placid and fathomless, but the high forehead of a thinker. His hair was white and luxuriant, falling in uncombed sweeps and folds to frame the broad cheeks and gently-smiling lips.

'I have heard the story of Llannef,' Selby said tentatively. And the other replied, 'Have you indeed, sir?' in a tone lacking surprise, as if it were the most natural thing in the world for a stranger to know the story.

After lunch, Selby took his coffee to a small iron table in the forecourt, a placid, very ordinary man in flannels and blue blazer, his spectacles aslant on his face, relaxing happily, the world he had left far away behind the tall cloud-wrapped mountains.

Children played in the sun, laughing and shouting, their voices clear and shrill. Their clothes were bright and clean, new-looking, almost, and he remarked on this when the landlord came blinking into the sun.

'All in their best today,' he explained to Selby, 'and a holiday from school. A celebration it is for everybody to mark the passing of old Gwan Hughes.'

Selby wondered idly who Gwan Hughes could have been that the anniversary of her death should be marked by a holiday. He put his thoughts into words, and the landlord looked mildly surprised.

'Early this morning, at dawn, it was, when she breathed her last; ailing for some time, and very old . . .'

And Selby, sipping his coffee, with the children's happy voices about him, thought how pleasant it was that death should be celebrated with laughter and a holiday instead of wreaths and mourning. It seemed so right. For a moment, the constant fear of his own death faded, and he could almost believe that here in Cwmbach he might find that which he had sought throughout the years.

Later, in the peace of his room, when he came to analyse his thoughts, he found it was because these people assumed death to be something that called for rejoicing that his own fears melted. For why should they be so happy, he reasoned, unless it was because they knew death to be something more than just the going out of a light?

After tea – an affair of freshly baked cake and hot buns dripping with butter – Selby tried to bring the conversation round to the story of Ifor Morgan and his village, but the landlord was politely evasive. But not because there was nothing to say about the man and the village that was never completed; Selby got the impression that he was reticent about discussing the matter simply because a 'foreigner' wouldn't understand.

The children were still playing in the street, and Selby watched them for a while, enjoying their holiday from school. From the school, his thoughts drifted to churches and he searched the surrounding roof-tops for the spire or steeple that would show its locality. But the village was flat, only the low slate roofs and the mountain slopes.

When the landlord came out, wiping his hands on a blue-edged towel, Selby asked him about a church or a chapel in Cwmbach, and the other smiled, shaking his head. The nearest chapel was beyond the mountains – at Bethesda, no less.

Then Selby got to thinking about the old lady who had just died. 'They will have to take her to Bethesda?' he wanted to know.

The landlord smiled again, almost pityingly, and changed the subject to salmon fishing, leaving Selby feeling that in some indefinable way he had been gently rebuffed.

With some idea of exploring the countryside, he went to the car, passed a rag over the windscreen and checked the petrol. The landlord watched the preparations with a slightly worried air.

'A run is it?' he asked. 'Perhaps as far back as Bethesda?'

Selby shook his head. 'I was thinking of following this road up into the mountains. There should be some excellent views from higher up.'

'I wouldn't advise it,' the other said carefully. 'The roads are bad, and one must be very careful. Night comes down quickly and there is a chance that you might lose yourself. And that, in the mountains, is a very bad thing.'

Selby levered himself behind the wheel and adjusted his glasses. He felt a little put out, even annoyed, at the insinuation that he was incapable of looking after himself.

'I'll risk it,' he said briefly, and started the car.

The other shouted something above the roar of the engine, and moving down the slope, Selby cupped his ear to catch the words.

'Look out – the fork – keep – to – left – mind you – right . . .'

He waved in acknowledgment of the scattered instructions, smiled a little to himself at the thought of the landlord's concern and swung out into the road.

The cottages fell behind, and the mountains crowded in for a while, then swept away again so that the valley spread itself out far below, a thing of brown and green squares, with the occasional glint and glitter of meandering streams. He stopped to admire the view, leaning out of the window, letting the salt-heavy breeze stir his hair, the tang of the sea on his lips. Life felt very good; there was a peace out here, between the sky and the valley, that he hadn't felt before.

He lay back against the soft upholstery, letting the calm engulf him, then dozed off, nodding gently, fat white fingers laced above the mound of his waist.

So Mr Pyle slept, suspended between Heaven and earth, with the seagulls crying high above, and only the peace of the mountain slopes to hear their calling.

When he awoke, refreshed, the sun was pulling itself down behind the highest peaks; the breeze had freshened and was cooler; dusk was slipping silently about him. The gulls had ceased their clamour, and the very earth seemed to hold its breath.

He started the car, debating for a moment whether or not to retrace his steps, but the lure of the winding road ahead was too strong; he set the bonnet into the cleft of the mountains.

After a while he came to where the road forked, three ways offering invitations, and he tried to remember the instructions flung after him by the anxious landlord. Had he to keep to the right or the left? But what matter when there would be time to explore each in their turn? Tonight it would be the road to the left, for that led up into the mountains, with the trees overhanging, and bushes and gorse thick on its verges.

The sun vanished, and night came down like a black cloak. The world was very still, the air sharp and clear. He breasted a slope where the rocky walls widened, and came on the scattered lights of a village in a hollow. He stopped then, drawing the car well into the side of the road, and unfolding his road map in the dim glow of the small roof light.

He managed to trace his path as far as Cwmbach itself, but then the road developed into series of dotted lines. He found the spot where he had slept overlooking the valley, and came upon a small village ahead. He strained over the name, holding the map to catch the light. Pengwyn it was called.

While he pored over the map, he caught sight of a movement, a flicker of movement in the driving mirror above his head. Someone was coming along the road behind, a nebulous white shape that resolved itself into the figure of a woman, dressed in a pale coloured frock and with a white shawl draped loosely over her head.

She walked with purpose, almost impatiently, with long, firm strides, her face to the village ahead, but turning to look at him as she passed the car, half-raising her arm in a gesture. She smiled into his eyes, the happy smile of a woman who smiled for the very pleasure of life; then she was ahead, a tall shadow in the lights of the car, vanishing into the blackness of the night.

Selby felt his heart warm to her gesture and smile. A woman who had passed, a stranger who had found time to offer her happiness. It was a woman going home, to a house that waited, with a husband and children to welcome her. He felt suddenly very envious of her happiness.

Her face was still bright in his mind when he started the car and slipped down the road, his headlamps cutting clear swathes of golden light. He found himself searching the night for her slim figure, with some idea at the back of his mind of offering a lift. But the houses were around him sooner than he had imagined, and then, for a brief moment he saw her, her hand on a gate, sharply outlined in the harsh glare of his lights.

He turned to look back over his shoulder, seeing how the cottage door was open and waiting to receive her; how a dark shadow in the golden oblong held out its arms to welcome. He felt absurdly pleased that he had seen the end of her journey.

He drove slowly through the comforting lights of cottages and houses, stopping finally in the friendly glow of the hotel. The bar was full, a place of noise and laughter. Selby sat in a corner, content to look on and, looking on, to become at one with the place. He felt tired, and the heavy warmth gave a dreamlike quality to the small room and friendly faces.

The landlord was a smiling grey-haired man whose features melted and blurred as he hovered with tray and glasses, speaking of the weather and the crops, of how things were in the valley.

'You have rooms?' Selby asked impulsively.

'But of course . . .' He seemed surprised at the question.

'Tomorrow, then,' Selby told him. 'I will come back tomorrow; my things are at a hotel in Cwmbach.'

'Perhaps it would be better if you were to stay,' the landlord offered gently. 'There may be no room tomorrow . . .'

He hesitated, then, but borrowed night-clothes offered little attraction. Also, the landlord of the 'Bryn Mawr' deserved consideration. It was only right and fair that he return, at least for the night. But afterwards – he was then prepared to spend the rest of his holiday in Pengwyn.

Mindful of the lateness of the hour, he rose and went out into the darkness. The landlord followed, standing by while he climbed behind the wheel. Then he said something which, at the time, held little sense.

'People don't usually go away again,' said he, shaking his head. 'There is something here that I don't understand.'

'I'll be back,' Selby told him sleepily, and drove away into the night.

At the top of the hill he stopped the car and turned to look back, refreshing his memory of the place. It lay there, a toy village in the dark cupped hand of the night. And as he watched, the lights winked out, one by one, until only a pool of darkness remained. The people of Pengwyn, it seemed, had gone to bed.

Back at the 'Bryn Mawr', the landlord seemed pleased to see him. His eyes asked a question while his hands were busy with tankards.

'I made it as far as Pengwyn,' Selby told him. 'A pleasant little place, too; I think I'll move along there tomorrow.' He yawned, it was getting late; the old clock above the counter was pointing to eleven.

'Just as you say, sir.' The landlord was politely disappointed. A burst of laughter came from the next room, and Selby looked pointedly at the clock. 'Your patrons keep late hours,' said he, 'later than the people of Pengwyn.'

'A special day, today,' the other explained. 'It is the sons of Gwan Hughes who drink to their mother's passing. It would be a pleasant gesture on your part if you were to join them. As for the licensing laws . . .' He smiled apologetically. 'On such a day one turns a blind eye.'

Selby went into the other room, noting in passing that a garland of flowers had been draped across the portrait of Ifor Morgan. It was like Christmas in July, but roses and lavender instead of holly.

They greeted him, three brown-faced, happy men, smiling and breaking off their singing to offer him a glass. 'For you to drink to our mother,' they told him, 'for she has left for the other place.'

There were others of the village too, men and women alike, all dressed in obvious Sunday finery, all smiling, all openly taking pleasure in the death of Gwan Hughes.

The sons were loquacious in drink, back-slapping and merry.

'And how old would your mother be?' Selby asked, to make conversation.

They discussed the matter earnestly amongst themselves, apparently never having given the matter much thought.

'Seventy-five,' the taller of the three hazarded.

'Not a day under eighty,' the one next to him contradicted. 'For you will remember she was putting money into the Trust right from the start . . .'

Selby felt a quickening of interest. 'The Trust?' he queried, but his words were lost in the good-natured argument that ringed the old lady's age. Comparative ages were being bandied, 'Sixteen years since Trevor here paid his first . . .' Twenty it'll be since I started, and that makes her all of eighty-six . . .'

Then a photograph, a thing of dog-ears and cracks, brown and faded, was produced from a bulky wallet, and Selby was invited to give his opinion. 'Taken some years ago, you will understand,' he was told, 'but you can see that she was a fine woman indeed.'

And as he stared at the placid, smiling face he knew that

he had seen it before. But not quite like that. Iron away the wrinkles from mouth and eyes, drape a white shawl over the hair . . .

'I have seen this woman before,' he told them. 'I have seen her this very evening. It was on the road to Pengwyn . . .'

And then a silence fell, with all the faces turned to his. They were puzzled and surprised. But the amazing thing was, he soon discovered, that they were not questioning the fact that he had seen their dead mother, but only that he had seen her on the way to Pengwyn.

The landlord, at his shoulder, asked gently, 'Tell us how you got to this village . . . Pengwyn, you call it.'

Selby told them, explaining how he had first fallen asleep, and then driven on until he reached the place where the road forked into three . . . And when he described this, they looked at each other, nodding wisely and significantly.

'And so you took the left-hand road, the old mountain road,' the landlord said, offering it as a statement rather than a question.

Selby agreed that he had taken the left-hand road.

'Pengwyn,' the other explained simply, 'lies to the right. It is a mining village, a place of slag heaps and tall chimneys. A place of coal-dust and filth.'

His voice was singing, his eyes aglow.

'You took the road to Morgan's village,' said he, 'to Llannef. And you saw Gwan Hughes on her way home . . .'

Selby Pyle lives in Cwmbach now; he has lived there for upwards of two years. Sooner or later, he believes that he will be approached to make his contribution to the Morgan Trust, and then he too will be on the list. So that when his time comes, the years will fall from his shoulders, and he in his turn will trace Gwan Hughes's steps along the road that leads to Llannef.

He has been, of course, to the fork in the road, and has seen for himself how it divides into two, with one leading to Pengwyn and the other to two mountain farms.

But there is a third road, an overgrown memory of a road

that was hardly ever made, and it leads up into the mountains. It is only the faintest of tracks, and Selby has followed it, coming to the crown of the hill, there to look down on the desolation of coarse grass and ivy-covered rubble which is all that remains of Ifor Morgan's village.

Like all the people of Cwmbach, he knows that sometimes the village is there – a place of lights and happiness – with a road that leads to it, an inviting, smooth highway. He knows, too, that once he has paid his deposit, he will be assured of a house in that village, and that one night the lights will shine out their welcome to him, as they did once before. But the next time he goes into the valley, it will be to stay.

And although he has finally completed his search for proof of life in the hereafter, he still feels regret that there should be a coldly impersonal thing as paying a deposit, and putting one's name down for a house.

He wonders, too, if there are likely to be mansions available, as well as cottages. But then, Selby Pyle, like most of us, is something of a snob at heart.

DEAD MAN'S CANDLE

In Wales, as in England, it is averred that the witches were in the habit of making what is called the 'dead man's candle'. According to the old superstition, so long as this taper continues to burn, the person who aroused the ire of the worker in 'black art' will have restless sleep and terrible dreams, or hideous nightmares.

The dead man's candle was placed in a dead man's hand, which in England and France was known as 'The Hand of Glory'. The Welsh say that the witches were always to be seen 'busy around the gallows tree'.

The dead man's hand was obtained thus: –

From a murderer's or any other corpse, the right hand was carefully severed, when the veins were bloodless, and before the flesh left the bones. It was then put into a piece of linen, while the witch counted the 'mystic count of seven'. She then named the seven 'governors of heaven' – Saturn, Jupiter, Mars, Venus, Mercury, the Sun, and the Moon. These ghastly fingers were then placed in an earthenware vessel, and covered with dragon-wort. Afterwards they were bleached in the sunshine.

The dead man's candle was made of the marrow of a murderer's or any other corpse, mixed with wax and Lapland sisame, the wick being made of the twisted hair of the dead.

From *Glimpses of Welsh Life and Character*

by Marie Trevelyan

WATER-HORSES AND SPIRITS OF THE MISTS

MARIE TREVELYAN

Weird and grotesque are the stories connected with the spectral lore of Wales.

Far back in the past the list of spectres included those of the waterfall, the forest, the mountain, and the valley. Taliesin, the bard of the fifth century, mentions the magic wand of Mathonwy, which, if found in the woodlands, would cause the fruit and flowers to appear more beautiful on the mysterious banks of the spectral waters.

Spectral stags and vast herds of spectral oxen were supposed to frequent the dense forests of Britain, and spectral horses lured huntsmen to leave the chase and go in pursuit of them.

The Ceffyl-dwr, or water-horse of Wales, was described as a beautiful but small creature, who, after tempting the unwary traveller to mount him, soared over river and mountain, then suddenly melted into thin air or mist, and threw his rider to destruction.

About fifty years ago people living in the rural districts firmly believed in the water-horse.

Near Glyn-Neath, a beautiful locality which is much frequented on account of the cascades caused by the rivers Perddyn, Little Neath, Mellte, and Hepste, a man, tired out after a long journey, lingered to rest in a shady nook.

A water-horse slowly came up from under the foaming cascade, shook the spray from its snow-white mane, and ascended the slope upon which the tired man rested. By-and-by the animal neighed, then snorted, and tossed its head proudly in the sunlight. The weary man was tempted to mount the fine creature, and this he found was remarkably easy of accomplishment. Soon he was safely astride the noble horse. Saddle and bridle he had not, but the grateful man felt the white mane of the animal to be an excellent substitute. He had not long mounted before he observed that the horse was going at an unusual speed. Moreover, he noticed that the horse's hoofs did not appear to touch the ground. For a time the astonished rider enjoyed the rapid rate at which the horse conveyed him, but after a while he became slightly alarmed. Wonder took the place of enjoyment, and soon terror supplanted both, as, up hill and down dale, the horse went with the speed of lightning. It was moonrise when he found himself thrown on the slope of a hill.

The shock of the fall was very great, and for a few moments he was completely dazed. Upon recovering his composure, he looked around for the horse which had carried him so swiftly and so far. To his surprise, the animal's graceful form became gradually indistinct. Then by slow degrees it appeared to merge in a vapoury cloud that hung low over the hill. By-and-by it vanished altogether. In the early night the man descended the slope, and after walking a mile or more he found himself in the ancient village of Llanddewi Brefi, Cardiganshire.

It was sunset when he left Glyn-Neath, and the long distance extending between that place and the remote village in Cardiganshire had been traversed in the short space of about an hour. [*C.D.*]

Another story of the kind comes from the banks of the Honddû.

Near the town of Brecon the remains of a Roman camp are still to be seen. It is supposed to have been formed by Ostorius Scapula, on the site of the British camp 'Caer Bannau,' from which the local Roman station was called 'Bannium.' This camp stands on the north bank of the River Honddû.

About a century ago a weary man was lured by a small grey water-horse from the camp to the edge of the river. Opportunity was too inviting to be lost, so the man mounted the horse, and in a very short space of time was set down on the banks of the Towy, not far from Carmarthen. Three days later the man was again lured by the small grey horse, and carried back to the Honddû – but, as the narrator said, 'in a worse state than when he left, for the Ceffyl-dwr had dragged him through mire and water, through brambles and briars, until he was scarcely knowable.' [*A. B.*]

The water-horse of the Honddû had a 'tormenting' reputation.

Flemingston, locally called Flimston, in the Vale of Glamorgan, was regarded as a favourite haunt of evil spirits in the form of water-horses. These creatures always appeared when people were benighted or lost on the desolate moorlands stretching for miles on each side of the River Thaw.

Sometimes the water-horse was luminous, and then more peculiar and bewildering.

In the early part of the nineteenth century an old man wended his way down these moors to Old Mill, near Aberthaw. It was a dark and cold night, late in December, and the traveller quickened his pace, for the clouds promised snow. When he had reached half-way to his destination, he was surprised to see, going slowly along before him, a solitary and small horse, ridden by a somewhat long-legged man.

The shape of the horse, from the ears to the tail, was distinctly outlined by a steady glow. The rider's boots, spurs, hunting-crop, and arms appeared tipped with light. The man was astonished to find that, although he used every effort to overtake the horse, he failed to do so.

Within an arm's length from the door of the Old Mill the

horse and its rider vanished mysteriously in the darkness that could almost be felt. When the old man entered the house he related his experiences. The people said he had seen the water-horse – the Ceffyl-dwr.

Before midnight the whole valley was flooded by an unusually high full-moon tide, and the traveller ever afterwards attributed his escape to the guidance of the water-horse, who lured him rapidly onward through the darkness to a place of safety.

It was said that clergymen and ministers of all denominations could ride the water-horse without falling until the desired destination was reached.

Two stories regarding the Ceffyl-dwr come from the Vale of Glamorgan.

The parson and parish clerk of Bouvilston, in the Vale, were walking homeward from Cardiff one dark night in the eighteenth century. Seeing a fine horse near the old bridge that spanned the River Ely, the parson said : 'Here is a stray : let us mount the animal, and get quicker home.'

'Well and good, sir,' said his companion; and they mounted, the parson in front and the clerk behind.

In silence, but swiftly, the horse reached the foot of the Tumble Hill, and they were ascending agreeably, when the clerk said : 'He is a good one to go, sir.'

With that the horse began to snort, and threatened to throw its riders. Again the clerk praised the horse, and then the animal pranced and reared dangerously.

'Hold your tongue, will you!' said the parson authoritatively, and the clerk remained silent.

The horse rapidly ascended the Tumble Hill, and soon went rushing through St Nicholas. As they approached Cottrell the clerk said : 'Darker and darker 'tis getting, sir. I do wish we were safe home!'

A moment later the clerk found himself in a ditch on the side of the road, while the horse whisked the parson in safety to his own door. When asked about this adventure, the clerk persisted the stray was the 'Ceffyl-dwr, and no other, for he carried the parson safe, but threw the clerk.'

The other 'old story' comes from Lydmoor, below Duffryn. An itinerant minister, wending his way past Lydmoor Mill, paused to rest beside the stream. He was then joined by one of the deacons of Trehill Calvinistic Methodist Chapel. Not far from the mill-pond at Duffryn the men saw a horse. Tired after a long walk, the minister suggested that he and his companion should mount, and so reach the chapel quicker.

'You can ride the horse home again tonight,' said the minister, 'and restore him to his owner, whoever he may be.'

'Ay, ay!' responded the deacon. 'It is the miller's horse, an' he'd be willing enough for you to ride him.'

So the men mounted, and the horse bore them rapidly up and down hill until they reached Tinkin's Wood, near which are several cromlechs.

Then the horse went on at a jog trot, to the discomfort of the riders.

'He is getting lazy and stubborn,' said the deacon; whereupon the horse reared fearfully. 'I can never hold on!' exclaimed the deacon; and he urged the minister to dismount, or allow him to do so.

Even as he spoke the horse again reared, and threw the deacon into the hedge.

The minister tried to alight and assist his friend, but the horse galloped away 'like lightning,' and the deacon had to walk to Trehill.

There the people assembled for service said: 'Serve thee right! He that talks on the back of the Ceffyl-dwr is sure to be thrown.'

The banks of the Towy, which flows through Carmarthen, were frequented by the Ceffyl-dwr.

A story was formerly told of a man who went down the Towy in an ancient coracle, but was seen returning home on a Ceffyl-dwr, which had eyes like balls of fire, and a snort like a blast. [*C. D.*]

In Carnarvonshire and several parts of North Wales the water-horse was supposed to fraternize with mountain ponies, and there is a tradition to the effect that the merlyns, or small horses known by that name, are the direct descendants of the Ceffyl-dwr.

It is singular to note that in Carnarvonshire, Montgomery, Merioneth, and Cardigan, the Ceffyl-dwr had the reputation of being able to transform itself into other shapes, and thus become a terror of the night. Sometimes it took the form of a goat, and rushed towards its victims with such force as to cause serious injury. In the Vale of Clwyd a Ceffyl-dwr delighted in leaping in the shape of a frog upon the backs of the people, clasping them with a fiendish embrace.

A Cardiganshire butter dealer of the old school declared that a Ceffyl-dwr followed him from the market town, and, in the form of a creature between a man and a goat, crushed him so severely with its superhuman weight that 'great black bruises' were to be seen 'for weeks' upon his shoulders and arms. [*O. S.*]

Near the town of Montgomery a Ceffyl-dwr, taking a hideous, indescribable shape, was accustomed to leap upon pedestrians and horsemen, almost crushing them to death with its weight. A man living in the wilds of the Rhondda, in Glamorgan, was riding down to Pontypridd early in the nineteenth century, when a Ceffyl-dwr, in the form of a squirrel, leaped between his shoulders. The creature clasped his neck so closely as to make the man gasp for breath. Then he was shaken and beaten so badly that the next day a mysterious illness assailed him, from which he never recovered, but lingered on in misery for nearly two years. [*J. R.*]

The stories of South Wales represent the Ceffyl-dwr generally as a small horse which allowed people to ride him. This animal was a temptation to weary pedestrians and benighted travellers. But in the stories of North Wales the Ceffyl-dwr was capable of varied transformations. In the North the horse was generally dark, with fiery eyes and a forbidding appearance. In the South he was often luminous, fascinating, and sometimes a winged steed.

The Ceffyl-dwr was frequently seen on the seashore, where

he appeared with a dapple-grey coat, or was very like the sand in colour. The old people said he could be identified by his hoofs being turned the wrong way. If anybody mounted him, he plunged with his rider into the foam. A man once caught a Ceffyl-dwr on the shores of Carmarthen Bay, and afterwards tried to break the creature in. By means of an artfully contrived bridle he led the animal home, and used it as a cart-horse. But one day the bridle became unfastened, and the Ceffyl-dwr darted with the cart and driver into the sea, and was never afterwards seen. [*C. D.*]

In some parts of Wales a Ceffyl-dwr, in the shape of a hulking or clumsy chestnut or piebald horse, trotted up and down the shore. The animal was seen in St Bride's Bay just after a storm. A farmer caught it, and put it to the plough. All went well for some weeks; then the Ceffyl-dwr, seized with an impulse, dragged both the plough and ploughman through the field at a furious pace, and reaching the shore, rushed into the sea, and was lost in the waves. [*O. S.*]

The Ceffyl-dwr, in the form of a huge and clumsy horse, was seen plunging up and down in the sea when thunderstorms were brewing, or before great gales. Sometimes its colour was grey or dappled white and brown, while in very stormy seasons it would be snowy white, and like the foam, or leaden-hued, harmonizing with the dark clouds and steel-coloured underwaves.

The Gwrach-y-rhibyn resembled the Irish banshee. Welshmen say this night-hag never troubles new families, only those whose ancestors have for long generations lived in the same place; in other words, the 'old stock.' This spectral form is described as having long black hair, black eyes, and swarthy countenance. Sometimes one of her eyes is grey and the other black. Both are deeply sunken and piercing. Her back was crooked, her figure was very thin and spare, and her pigeon-breasted bust was concealed by a sombre scarf. Her trailing robes were black. She was sometimes seen with long flapping wings that fell heavily at her sides, and occasionally she went flying low down along watercourses, or around hoary mansions. Frequently the flapping of her leathern bat-like wings could be heard against the window-panes.

St Donat's Castle, on the seashore of Glamorgan, has always been inhabited since the coming of the Normans into Wales, even though occasionally it was not in the owner's occupation. The Stradlings were holders of it from Norman times until the middle of the eighteenth century, when it was the subject of a romantic law-suit, which lasted over fifty years. The heir of the Stradling family went on a tour with his friend Tyrwhitt, and before starting it was agreed by the two young men that if during their travels anything should befall the other, the survivor was to inherit the deceased's estates. Both were rich, and their estates valuable. In the meantime the father of Thomas Stradling died, and the absent heir came into possession of the St Donat's estate. In 1738 Thomas Stradling was killed in a duel at Montpellier, in France, and Tyrwhitt, of Wiltshire, according to agreement, became the owner of St Donat's. The Stradling family believed the rightful heir had been the victim of foul play, and laid claim to the possessions. During the long years of litigation the Tyrwhitts let the castle in succession to highly respectable people, from the descendants of whom many stories of the place have been obtained.

In the lore connected with the castle the Gwrach-y-rhibyn appears. One night early in the nineteenth century a stranger who was visiting the family resident in the castle, distinctly heard a moaning and wailing sound close under his window. It was like 'the pitiful sound of a woman in the greatest possible agony.' The visitor ventured to look out, but was alarmed by the flapping of wings against the lattice, and a rattling noise like that of talons. In the morning he told his host and hostess of his experiences, and they said it was the Gwrach-y-rhibyn, who always frequented the castle, and lamented the death of the last of the Stradlings in the direct line. They said that sometimes this mysterious figure wandered through the empty and silent rooms of the disused part of the castle, and the sounds of her lamentation were 'enough to turn one's blood to ice.' Once the Gwrach-y-rhibyn traversed the village from end to end, and in the dim uncertain twilight of a November evening her flowing robes and out-stretched arms were 'against the wind,' and caused a 'roaring noise.' She was once seen beating the boundaries of the whole estate, and was accompanied by black hounds with red eyes and horrible fangs.

Near a small crek that runs into the land from Oxwich Bay stand the ruins of Pennard Castle, which was built on the site of a stronghold of Danish rovers. The castle was the property of a Norman lord, and the old story goes that it was built in a single night by a Welsh sorcerer, who in this way saved his life from threatened imprisonment and assassination by the Normans. Around this castle the Gwrach-y-rhibyn often wandered, and was seen and heard by people so late as the first half of the nineteenth century. People along the country-side used formerly to say that if anybody slept for the night among the ruins of Pennard Castle he would be bewitched. It was solemnly stated that centuries ago a man once slept in the ruins after being told not to do so. During the night, the Gwrach-y-rhibyn attacked him violently, and almost 'left him for dead.' He was found in the morning quite unconscious, with bruises on his body, scratches upon his face, and other evidences of maltreatment. When he 'came to himself' he described the terrible appearance of the hag who attacked him, and said she 'clawed' him just as an eagle might have done. Then she 'pecked' at his body and beat him. The man went home to Carmarthen, and ever afterwards was bewitched, as the people near Pennard Castle said he would be 'for all time.' [*A. B. and O. S.*]

Beaupré Castle, on the banks of the River Thaw, near Cowbridge, Glamorgan, became uninhabitable in the eighteenth century, when a residence known as New Beaupré was erected. It originally belonged to the Welsh Seisyllt family, from whom the present Lord Salisbury is said to be descended, the family name Cecil being a corruption of Seisyllt. Beaupré was restored by the Normans, and descended by heirship to the Bassett family, who came into possession about the year 1200. Later on it was sold to the Edmunds family, and subsequently to the

Treharnes of St Hilary, from whom it was bought by a solicitor. During the Edmunds ownership, and while the Treharnes possessed the castle, the Gwrach-y-rhibyn frequented the place. There was an old story prevalent that the hag had been seen rising up out of the River Thaw, and wringing her hands and flapping her bat-like wings in the twilight. She also seemed to have a grievance against New Beaupré, for late in the eighteenth century she was seen and heard in the grounds. Early in the nineteenth century workmen staying in the neighbourhood declared they had seen the Gwrach-y-rhibyn among the ruins of the old castle, and the wailing and sobbing were painful to hear. Soon all the neighbourhood rang with the story, and as time passed the hag became more persistent. When the solicitor bought the estate he heard the story of the Gwrach-y-rhibyn, and was much interested in it. A year or two before this owner's death the following story was told by an old man in the Vale of Glamorgan: Above the entrance doorway of the castle a panel bears the Bassett arms and motto, *Gwell angau na chwilydd* ('Rather death than shame'). The old man was doing some work near this door, and it was twilight. While busily engaged, he heard a low, sad wailing sound wandering around the courtyard, and immediately opposite, in the grand porch of the castle, he saw a shadowy figure standing wringing its hands and flitting in and out like somebody in distress. The spectator crossed the courtyard and approached the porch, and as he did so the figure vanished. Curiosity prompted him to venture farther in, and as he went a voice seemed to whisper in his ears, 'Lost! lost! lost!' He looked around, but could not see anybody. Quietly he re-entered the porch, and the wailing, moaning, and sobbing began again. Then the figure with the waving hands reappeared, and the old man distinctly heard a sweet but sad voice, in wailing accents, crying: 'Restore! restore! restore!' The old man went home, and the next day told the solicitor who owned the castle the story of the Gwrach-y-rhibyn. 'I know all about it,' said the gentleman, who was one of the kindest-hearted in Glamorgan. 'Strange voices often come from the past, and act as monitors for the future. I know all about it.' The old man understood that the owner also had seen and heard the Gwrach-y-rhibyn in her wanderings and wailings and whisperings around picturesque old Beaupré. Whether this story was true or not, it is certain that the then owner, Mr Daniel Jones, left the Beaupré estate by will to Captain Bassett, a direct descendant of the original owners, in whose family it still remains. The grand old porch (designed by Inigo Jones, and built by Gwylim Twrch) of Beaupré is one of the 'show places' of the Vale of Glamorgan. It is said that at the castle of Beaupré arrangements and terms were made to compel King John to sign the Magna Charta. Sir Philip Bassett of that period was afterwards Lord Chief Justice of England. [*Family Collection.*]

The Caerphilly swamp, through which the stream Nant-y-Gledyr flows, was frequented by the Gwrach-y-rhibyn. This swamp, when the river was dammed up, formed a lake, and was used for the defence of the fortress-castle of Caerphilly, where the powerful De Clares dwelt. In the last half of the eighteenth century the hag was seen by many living in the district. An old man, who remembered his father's version of the story, said that in rainy seasons the stream overflowed the marshy ground, and from the midst of the lake formed thereby, the Gwrach-y-rhibyn arose, and dipped herself up and down in the water. From her bat-like wings, her long black hair, and talon-like fingers the water dropped sparkling in the moonlight. Each time she arose from the water she would wring her hands and moan, or utter a long-drawn wail, or a groan which was terrible to hear. Then, suddenly flapping her wings, she would fly to the castle and take refuge within its walls. Boys and men were known to watch the hag, and used every endeavour to catch her, but without success. The old man said his father had seen her several times, and was afraid of the rainy weather and the gloomy swamp. Sometimes the hag wandered up and down beside the stream in dry weather. His father had seen her. It was 'as true as the Bible – iss, indeed!' he said. [*C. D.*]

Stories about the Brenin Llwyd, the Grey King, or Monarch

of the Mist, were told in most of the mountainous districts. In the North he was described as being very mighty and powerful. He was represented as sitting among the mountains, robed in grey clouds and mist, and woe to anybody who was caught in his clutches! Snowdon and the ranges of it, Cader Idris, Plinlimmon, and other lofty places, were his favourite haunts. In the South he was regarded as 'hungering' for victims, and children were warned not to venture too high up the mountains, lest the Brenin Llwyd should seize them. So late as the first half of the nineteenth century, whenever an adult or a child was lost on Gellionen, near Alltwen, or on the Garth Maelog, Glamorgan, people said the Brenin Llwyd had seized its prey. An old woman said that when she was a child, and visited relatives at Llantrisant, Glamorgan, the children believed the Brenin Llwyd lived among the local mountains. She said that many a time she shuddered when they ascended to the mineral wells on the Smaelog, and was glad to come down, because the people and children warned everybody not to linger late, for the Brenin Llwyd would be after them. She was further told that there was no trusting him, for sometimes on the brightest summer evening he would come suddenly and draw them into his clutches. [*O. S.*]

A resident in the North said that formerly the old guides among the Snowdon ranges were fond of telling stories about the Brenin Llwyd, who came stealthily and silently up through the ravines, or sat waiting among lonely peaks to imprison the unwary. In the childhood of those old men few cared to make long ascents, and even the guides were nervous occasionally, when the old people talked in the fireside corners about the ever-silent and gloomy but treacherous Brenin Llwyd, whose movements were never heard when he came to take his prisoners.

THE TOLLING BELL

In the old fifth century university town of Llantwit Major, the passing bell is said to toll without the touch of human hands, before a death in the parish. The bell is frequently heard tolling over, or in the direction of the house where an inmate will soon die. Some of the people there say that before a funeral, noises and commotion are always heard in the churchyard where St Iltutus was buried, and that still, if anyone has the courage to look through the keyhole of the church door, on one of the *Teir nos ysprydion* – 'three spirit nights' – he will see the spectral forms of those who are to depart this life during the year. Blaenporth, Cardiganshire, is also noted for the passing bell tolling before a death in the parish. If it gives three tolls at noon or midnight, somebody of influence will die.

The 'three spirit nights', when, according to Welsh tradition, the souls of the departed are permitted to return to earth, are the eves of All Saints, Christmas, and the New Year.

From *Glimpses of Welsh Life and Character*

by Marie Trevelyan

BE THIS HER MEMORIAL

CARADOC EVANS

Mice and rats, as it is said, frequent neither churches nor poor men's homes. The story I have to tell you about Nanni – the Nanni who was hustled on her way to prayer-meeting by the Bad Man, who saw the phantom mourners bearing away Tom Tybach's coffin, who saw the Spirit Hounds and heard their moanings two days before Isaac Penparc took wing – the story I have to tell you contradicts that theory.

Nanni was religious; and she was old. No one knew how old she was, for she said that she remembered the birth of each person that gathered in Capel Sion; she was so old that her age had ceased to concern.

She lived in the mud-walled, straw-thatched cottage on the steep road which goes up from the Garden of Eden, and ends at the tramping way that takes you into Cardigan town; if you happen to be travelling that way you may still see the roofless walls which were silent witnesses to Nanni's great sacrifice – a sacrifice surely counted unto her for righteousness, though in her search for God she fell down and worshipped at the feet of a god.

Nanni's income was three shillings and ninepence a week. That sum was allowed her by Abel Shones, the officer for Poor Relief, who each pay-day never forgot to remind the crooked, wrinkled, toothless old woman how much she owed to him and God.

'If it was not for me, little Nanni,' Abel was in the habit of telling her, 'you would be in the House of the Poor long ago.'

At that remark Nanni would shiver and tremble.

'Dear heart,' she would say in the third person, for Abel was a mighty man and the holder of a proud office, 'I pray for him night and day.'

Nanni spoke the truth, for she did remember Abel in her prayers. But the workhouse held for her none of the terrors it holds for her poverty-stricken sisters. Life was life anywhere, in cottage or in poorhouse, though with this difference: her liberty in the poorhouse would be so curtailed that no more would she be able to listen to the spirit-laden eloquence of the Respected Josiah Bryn-Bevan. She helped to bring Josiah into the world; she swaddled him in her own flannel petticoat; she watched him going to and coming from school; she knitted for him four pairs of strong stockings to mark his going out into the world as a farm servant; and when the boy, having obeyed the command of the Big Man, was called to minister to the congregation of Capel Sion, even Josiah's mother was not more vain than Old Nanni. Hence Nanni struggled on less than three shillings and ninepence a week, for did she not give a tenth of her income to the treasury of the Capel? Unconsciously she came to regard Josiah as greater than God: God was abstract; Josiah was real.

As Josiah played a part in Nanni's life, so did a Seller of Bibles play a minor part in the last few days of her travail. The man came to Nanni's cottage the evening of the day of the rumour that the Respected Josiah Bryn-Bevan had received a call from a wealthy sister church in Aberystwyth. Broken with grief, Nanni, the first time for many years, bent her stiffened limbs and addressed herself to the living God.

'Dear little Big Man,' she prayed, 'let not your son bach religious depart.'

Then she recalled how good God had been to her, how He had permitted her to listen to His son's voice; and another fear struck her heart.

'Dear little Big Man,' she muttered between her blackened gums, 'do you now let me live to hear the boy's farewell words.'

At that moment the Seller of Bibles raised the latch of the door.

'The Big Man be with this household,' he said, placing his pack on Nanni's bed.

'Sit you down,' said Nanni, 'and rest yourself, for you must be weary.'

'Man,' replied the Seller of Bibles, 'is never weary of well-doing.'

Nanny dusted for him a chair.

'No, no; indeed now,' he said; 'I cannot tarry long, woman. Do you not know that I am the Big Man's messenger? Am I not honoured to take His word into the highways and byways, and has He not sent me here?'

He unstrapped his pack, and showed Nanni a gaudy volume with a clasp of brass, and containing many coloured prints; the pictures he explained at hazard: here was a tall-hatted John baptising, here a Roman-featured Christ praying in the

Garden of Gethsemane, here a frock-coated Moses and the Tablets.

'A Book,' said he, 'which ought to be on the table of every Christian home.'

'Truth you speak, little man,' remarked Nanni. 'What shall I say to you you are asking for it?'

'It has a price far above rubies,' answered the Seller of Bibles. He turned over the leaves and read: ' "The labourer is worthy of his hire." Thus is it written. I will let you have one copy – one copy only – at cost price.'

'How good you are, dear me!' exclaimed Nanni.

'This I can do,' said the Seller of Bibles, 'because my Master is the Big Man.'

'Speak you now what the cost price is.'

'A little sovereign, that is all.'

'Dear, dear; the Word of the little Big Man for a sovereign!'

'Keep you the Book on your parlour table for a week. Maybe others who are thirsty will see it.'

Then the Seller of Bibles sang a prayer; and he departed.

Before the week was over the Respected Josiah Bryn-Bevan announced from his pulpit that in the call he had discerned the voice of God bidding him go forth into the vineyard.

Nanni went home and prayed to the merciful God:

'Dear little Big Man, spare me to listen to the farewell sermon of your saint.'

Nanni informed the Seller of Bibles that she would buy the Book, and she asked him to take it away with him and have written inside it an inscription to the effect that it was a gift from the least worthy of his flock to the Respected Josiah Bryn-Bevan, D.D., and she requested him to bring it back to her on the eve of the minister's farewell sermon.

She then hammered hobnails into the soles of her boots, so as to render them more durable for tramping to such capels as Bryn-Bevan happened to be preaching in. Her absences from home became a byword, occurring as they did in the hay-making season. Her labour was wanted in the fields. It was the property of the community, the community which paid her three shillings and ninepence a week.

One night Sadrach Danyrefail called at her cottage to commandeer her services for the next day. His crop had been on the ground for a fortnight, and now that there was a prospect of fair weather he was anxious to gather it in. Sadrach was going to say hard things to Nanni, but the appearance of the gleaming-eyed creature that drew back the bolts of the door frightened him and tied his tongue. He was glad that the old woman did not invite him inside, for from within there issued an abominable smell such as might have come from the boiler of the witch who one time lived on the moor. In the morning he saw Nanni trudging towards a distant capel where the Respected Josiah Bryn-Bevan was delivering a sermon in the evening. She looked less bent and not so shrivelled up as she did the night before. Clearly, sleep had given her fresh vitality.

Two Sabbaths before the farewell sermon was to be preached Nanni came to Capel Sion with an ugly sore at the side of her mouth; repulsive matter oozed slowly from it, forming into a head, and then coursing thickly down her chin on to the shoulder of her black cape, where it glistened among the beads. On occasions her lips tightened, and she swished a hand angrily across her face.

'Old Nanni,' folks remarked while discussing her over their dinner-tables, 'is getting as dirty as an old sow.'

During the week two more sores appeared; the next Sabbath Nanni had a strip of calico drawn over her face.

Early on the eve of the farewell Sabbath the Seller of Bibles arrived with the Book, and Nanni gave him a sovereign in small money. She packed it up reverently, and betook herself to Sadrach Danyrefail to ask him to make the presentation.

At the end of his sermon the Respected Josiah Bryn-Bevan made reference to the giver of the Bible, and grieved that she was not in the Capel. He dwelt on her sacrifice. Here was a Book to be treasured, and he could think of no one who would treasure it better than Sadrach Danyrefail, to whom he would hand it in recognition of his work in the School of the Sabbath.

In the morning the Respected Josiah Bryn-Bevan, making a tour of his congregation, bethought himself of Nanni. The thought came to him on leaving Danyrefail, the distance betwixt which and Nanni's cottage is two fields. He opened the door and called out:

'Nanni.'

None answered.

He entered the room. Nanni was on the floor.

'Nanni, Nanni!' he said. 'Why for you do not reply to me? Am I not your shepherd?'

There was no movement from Nanni. Mishtir Bryn-Bevan went on his knees and peered at her. Her hands were clasped tightly together, as though guarding some great treasure. The minister raised himself and prised them apart with the ferrule of his walking-stick. A roasted rat revealed itself. Mishtir Bryn-Bevan stood for several moments spellbound and silent; and in the stillness the rats crept boldly out of their hiding places and resumed their attack on Nanni's face. The minister, startled and horrified, fled from the house of sacrifice.

THE BLACK LADY OF BOVERTON

Not far from St Athan is Boverton, supposed to be the Bovium of the Romans. The Castle of Boverton was a British Stronghold, afterwards occupied by the Romans and Normans. In the reign of Richard I, it was the property of the Earl of Gloucester, whose daughter Hadwisa became the wife of Prince John. When, ten years later, John divorced Hadwisa of Gloucester so that he could marry Isabella of Angouleme, his wife, who has been described as amiable and affectionate, retired to the seclusion of Boverton Castle.

Early in the nineteenth century men were employed to dismantle part of this castle. One dark hazy day they saw a tall, shadowy female figure, dressed in deep widow's mourning of antique design. Her face was scarcely visible, but her long dark hair fell in neatly braided tresses down to her waist. She wandered from room to room in a slow disconsolate manner, and occasionally her sobs and sighs broke the silence. At first the workmen were greatly frightened, but as during the progress of the work they frequently saw the apparition little heed was taken of it. One of the men mentioned the circumstance to a very aged person in the district, and was told: 'Oh, she is Wissie, the King's widow. I've often seen her.' May not this dark lady have been Hadwisa of Gloucester?

When the dismantling of the old castle was completed the dark apparition vanished, but for long years afterwards people declared the black lady haunted Boverton Castle.

From *Folk-lore and Folk-stories of Wales* by Marie Trevelyan

THE LOST GOLD MINE

HAZEL F. LOOKER

South Wales is famous for its steam-coal and anthracite; old lead mines are scattered among the hills of mid-Wales, and there is gold, too. True, Wales has never known a gold rush, as there is far too little gold for that, but the fever can take hold of anyone, and once it gets into the blood it drives a man on until he finds gold or dies in the attempt.

There was only one small hotel in Tresaint (pronounced Sant); it had about eight bedrooms, and kept a very good table. There was also pony trekking in the village, and some of the trekkers stayed at the hotel, while others either camped out or found accommodation in the neighbouring farms and cottages.

Sue Milbrook and her two friends, Richard Price and Tim Westgate, had booked early, so they had rooms at the hotel, and, having travelled down in Sue's car, were all set to enjoy their last holiday together. They had just completed their college courses, and each would soon be embarking on his or her own career.

Sue was a good rider and had her own pony back home, but the two boys had yet to discover the joys of horsemanship. Sue had worked up their enthusiasm, telling them of the views from the hills which no motorist ever saw, of the peace that comes when one is seated on a sure-footed pony following some moorland track, and the fun with fellow trekkers.

'You need proper riding breeches,' she said. 'That's important, otherwise you'll get sore between the knees if you are riding properly. Good boots, too, because you often have to "squelch" through bogs. Some people wear riding hats, but I'm not taking mine, it gives me a headache. I always wear gloves though – stops my hands from getting sore and dirty.'

Over the washbasin in each bedroom hung a card giving information of meal times and places of interest in the locality. Tresaint, it informed them, meant Three Saints, so called because three Celtic Saints had rested here on their way to found a priory. The stone on which they sat could still be seen, hollowed out where each Saint had rested. There was also a gold mine worked in Roman times which was worth a visit.

Tim, who had taken Economic Geography as one of his special subjects at college, was interested in rocks. In fact, he had often thought of becoming a geologist and getting a job prospecting for some big company. His aim was to get rich quick if he could, and, while not being exactly mean, he hated parting with money; at the end of term he was always the one left with something in the bank. This old gold mine interested him, and he made a mental note to visit it at the first opportunity.

While waiting for the others to join him in the bar before dinner that evening he asked the landlord how far it was to the gold mine.

'Oh, not far,' the landlord replied. 'You go down to the bridge, turn left at the next fork opposite the chapel, then go on up the lane till you come to a big farm, and right opposite there you'll see the Saints' stone – it's on the grass verge. You can't miss it.'

'I'm not interested in the stone,' Tim retorted. 'Where's the gold mine?'

'If you'll give me a chance, I'll tell you,' the landlord frowned. 'Climb up a steep bank that's just behind the stone, and over the top you'll see the old workings.'

'Thank you,' said Tim, and finished his beer just as his friends appeared.

'Let's go in to dinner right away,' he urged, 'then we'll have time for a stroll before it gets too dark.'

As soon as dinner was over he led the way in the direction indicated by the landlord, but after some twenty minutes Sue said: 'Let's go back now, I'm tired after all that driving.'

'It isn't far now,' Tim insisted.

'What isn't far?' Richard asked.

'The gold mine, I want to have a look at it.'

'Oh, all right,' Sue agreed with some reluctance, 'but you haven't been driving all day as I have.'

They turned a bend in the lane, and after descending an incline came to what appeared to be a village green; to the left of this were cultivated fields, and on the right they found the stone. It was hollowed out into three seats.

Tim gave the stone a kick. 'Three Saints indeed,' he said scornfully, 'I've seen stones like this in Cornwall. The old tin miners used them for washing the stuff they brought out of the mine, and in time water wore hollows in the stone, like these, and then they turned it over and used the other side.'

He took a run up the high bank, and found himself looking down into a kind of amphitheatre. The bank of debris formed a half-circle on the mountainside, and at the bottom Tim saw the entrance to the mine. It was a tunnel hewn out of the solid rock, and appeared to be about two feet deep in water.

'It must have taken them ages to cut into that rock with their primitive tools,' said Sue.

'They were great engineers, the Romans,' Richard remarked,

'I mean, think of all those marvellous aqueducts they built.'

Tim did not comment. His one desire was to get down into that tunnel and examine the rock, but he knew it was no use asking the others to wait any longer, so he decided to come again on his own and have a really good look round.

Next morning they found the paddock where the ponies were being saddled bustling with trekkers clad in every conceivable type of riding kit, ranging from the immaculate to jeans-and-Wellington-boots. Sue helped her friends to saddle and bridle their ponies, and showed them how to tighten the girth because, as she explained; 'Ponies blow out their bellies when you put the saddle on, and if you don't tighten up it might slip round and you'll perhaps end up under the horse's belly.'

At last they were ready, and set off through the village looking rather like Chaucer's pilgrims on their way to Canterbury. Sue laughed as she watched some novices cling to their saddle with one hand, while others held the reins high and tight, making the poor ponies' necks arch.

'Never have so many suffered so much at the hands of those who know so little,' she misquoted.

However, confidence grew as they journeyed on, for Twm Trek, as the guide was called, took it easy on this first day. Soon they were up on the mountain tracks, relaxed and able to chat with one another as the sure-footed animals picked their way over the rough stones or boggy places. Tim caught up with the guide and offered him a cigarette.

'It's not too bad up here today,' said Twm as he lit up. 'We've had a lot of rain lately, and after a wet spring things can be a bit dicey sometimes. I've seen trekkers come off in a bog and come out covered in black mud. They've had to let it dry and then peel it off in chunks.' He chuckled. 'These little ponies are good, though, they can pick their own way if you let them. Horses would be no good up here, sir.'

Tim, after a while, remarked casually: 'The old gold mine – am I to understand it is completely worked out?'

'Yes, indeed,' Twm nodded. 'The seam was worked out long

ago, but they do say it grew richer and richer, then suddenly stopped. No more gold, just plain old rock.'

It was Tim's turn to nod. 'The rock must have split and one part slipped down. But surely with all the modern instruments we have nowadays it should be possible to find the seam again?'

'Oh, lots of people have tried from time to time,' Twm said, 'but none of them had any luck. Though if the old tale be true there is a way of finding it.'

'How?' asked Tim breathlessly.

The guide did not answer for some little while, then he began to speak in a quiet tone as though he were revealing some secret; like a man reluctantly uncovering a family skeleton to the morbid gaze of a stranger. 'Now look you, this yarn has been passed down from father to son, and maybe it's all eyewash, although there are those today who swear it's all true. But it is said that a long time ago the rich seam was found, and work started on it, then something happened. A terrible disaster like, all the miners died, nobody knows how, but no living thing came back, neither men nor ponies – they used ponies like these to cart the stuff away, see.'

'How dreadful.' Tim felt he could do no more than make some such remark.

'Yes,' the guide nodded, 'if it was true, it must have been dreadful. But this is the story you wanted to hear. They, the old ones you understand, say that on some nights if you go up the lane by the chapel you'll see the ponies making their way to the new seam. If a man wants gold bad enough, all he has to do is to follow them.'

'And has anyone ever followed them?' Tim inquired after a while.

'Yes,' Twm said shortly, then added 'or so it is said.'

'And . . .?'

The guide turned his head and looked the young man full in the face.

'They never came back.'

Tim, despite his modern, matter-of-fact outlook, felt a shiver run down his spine, then he laughed.

'Sure you don't believe any of this?'

Twm nudged his horse forward.

'Maybe I don't,' he said, and terminated the conversation by riding a little way ahead, leaving a very thoughtful young man behind him.

Next morning Tim announced he was not joining the trek.

'I'm disgusted with you,' said Sue, 'giving up so soon. The stiffness will wear off once you get back into the saddle.'

'It's not that,' Tim said, 'I promise I'll come tomorrow, but there's something I must do today.'

'Please yourself,' Sue walked away, her head held high, for she liked people to do what she wanted, and the boys, being of an easy going nature, usually followed her lead. Tim grimaced, then set off in the direction of the old gold mine. He climbed the bank, then trudged down the incline to the tunnel cut into the mountainside; the water was fully two feet deep, clear as a washed window pane, but, as he found out once he had removed his shoes and socks and waded in, extremely cold. He reached up and tried to pull a sample of rock from the low roof, but he could find no loose fragments. Spotting a jagged stone lying on a narrow ledge, he used this as a hammer, and finally managed to collect a few good specimens. They were brownish-yellow in colour, but there was no suggestion they might contain gold ore. He followed the course of the tunnel some twenty yards into the mountainside, using the torch he had thoughtfully brought with him, but here he was brought to a halt by a fall of rock which completely blocked the passage.

He retraced his footsteps and, once back in the open air, removed his drenched trousers and laid them out in the sun to dry, then sat down and tried to reason out just where the new seam, always supposing it existed, could have been located. It could possibly have been somewhere beyond that fall of rock; that being the case, without elaborate machinery he had no hope of reaching it. This could well have been the disaster that had overcome the long-dead miners, a sudden cave-in, burying men and ponies. But if that had happened, surely some effort would have been made to get them out, or recover their remains. No, he was certain the new workings were farther afield, but the question was, where? On one side there was the mountain, over to the east was a vast swamp, to the north, open moorland. That must be the answer, out there in that desolate waste; the home of the moorhen, where the occasional tree bowed its head to the prevailing wind as though begging alms from the sun, and the rough heather-clad earth glowered up at the benign sky. Tim Westgate rose quickly, pulled on his still damp trousers, discarded his usually much-valued commonsense, and went out on to the moor. The gold fever was in his bloodstream.

He wandered a long way that day, climbing hills, peering into grass-choked hollows, never really believing he would find that which he sought, but unable to give up the search which his reasoning powers vainly tried to tell him was a complete waste of time. He lunched at a moorland inn, a small dismal place ruled over by a dour landlord who seemed to resent this stranger demanding refreshment, then went forth again on his seemingly endless quest.

Night was sending its dark shadow over the moor before he returned to the realms of sanity; he looked over to the western horizon and saw the flaming rim of the sun, felt the icy fingers of the night wind and tasted fear. To be lost on the moor at night was no joke, and he began to make his way towards the now distant mountain, praying that he might reach the village before complete darkness fell. In fact his fears were groundless, a full moon was painting the old chapel with a silver glow when he entered the lane, footsore, tired to the state of exhaustion, but thankful his journey was almost over.

'I was mad,' he told himself, 'mad. As though one could hope to find gold in twentieth-century Wales.'

He passed the chapel and had reached the end of the lane when he heard the sound. A soft padding, then a clip-clop, followed by the rattle of harness. Tim began to shiver; he felt the short hairs on the back of his neck begin to rise as he remembered the story told to him by Twm Trek.

The ponies came out from nowhere. First the head, then the shoulders, finally a complete pony emerged from a position roughly in the centre of the lane; it was as though it had come through an invisible curtain. Tim flattened himself against the wall as another pony followed the first, then another; presently a long file were trudging up the lane, some carrying picks and trenching tools strapped to their backs, others bearing empty sacks or long, sharp-pointed stakes. Tim was shivering with terror, but somewhere, from the back of his fear-crazed brain, a thought sprang into being and would not be ignored. If he were to follow this phantom file, would they not lead him to the new seam? A vision of himself at the head of a gold mining company; wealth, power, position – fear began to recede before a rising lust for gold.

The last pony passed him, and almost against his will Tim left the security of the wall and began to follow the ghostly line. The clink of harness, the soft pad of hoofs, an occasional snort, Tim could scarcely believe this was not a file of living animals wending their way towards the open moor. Then, with another blast of icy fear, he realised they cast no shadow; the full moon highlighted the brown or black rumps, gilded the metal trappings on harness or trenching tools, but there were no silhouettes, no evidence of solid bodies intruding between moonlight and earth.

They skirted the lower slopes of the mountain, passed the old mine entrance, then proceeded on down an incline towards a cluster of wind-bowed trees.

'Downhill, of course.' Excitement bubbled in Tim's fevered brain. 'They did not try to follow the seam deeper into the mountain, they went back to its source. The beginning.'

The first pony disappeared into the deep shadow that lurked beneath the trees; the others followed, seemingly guided by invisible hands. When Tim at last entered the eerie gloom he found his progress was hampered by dense undergrowth. It seemed there was an active force trying to hold him back;

brambles clung to his legs, encircled his waist, and he swore as he wrenched himself free, only to bark his shins on a fallen branch, walk into a low bush, whose whippy branches seemed determined to beat him back. All the while he could hear the ponies trudging sedately ahead. Once, when a gap in the overhead treetops permitted the moonlight a sparse entrance, he had a glimpse of the last animal moving effortlessly through a thick bush.

When he emerged from that nightmare wood, his face and hands were covered with weals and scratches, but he gave a joyful cry when he saw the line of ponies crossing what appeared to be a smooth, grass-carpeted expanse of open country. They were now some forty yards away, and Tim broke into a run, determined to catch them up, certain that by now he must be within reach of his Mecca – the new workings.

The earth reached up and clutched his feet; there was an awful sucking sound, an obscene squelching, and he began to sink down into that treacherous green carpet. He struggled, an action that only made his predicament worse, for now the mire was up to his thighs, and the sucking, squelching sounds were like evil chuckles as the bog drew him deeper into its embrace. Even now he could not entirely forget the receding ponies. They too were going down into the bog, but they were walking as though down an incline, and Tim laughed aloud, a mad shriek as the last pony disappeared from view.

'So that's where it is. Under thirty or forty feet of bloody, life-sucking bog.'

He was down to his waist when he began to scream, long drawn out shrieks that ran out across the moor, and the moon gazed down at him with her cold, silver-hued face, like a beautiful woman disdainfully ignoring the pleading of a discarded lover. The mire had reached his armpits before he again heard the sound of approaching ponies' hoofs, and he screamed his terror-inspired rage.

'You've got me, there's no need to come back.'

'Tim!'

The voice came out of yesterday; from the far-off world of

sanity, where young men did not follow ghostly ponies and flounder in Welsh bogs. He turned his head and saw Sue and Richard standing a few yards away; the boy's face was strained and white, but Sue wore an expression of grim determination. She snapped:

'Richard, quick, fetch a long branch!'

'But . . .' Richard could not tear his terror-stricken gaze from Tim's three-quarter submerged form.

Sue shouted again: 'Don't stand there, fetch a long branch!'

After Richard had departed, she spoke soothingly to Tim.

'Don't move. Keep absolutely still. It's your only chance.'

It was fifteen minutes before they pulled him out, for the bog was reluctant to part with a victim, and when he finally lay on firm ground, Tim gasped out his thanks.

'I knew something had gone wrong when you didn't return at sunset,' Sue said. 'Suddenly I remembered the bog, though why on earth you should want to come down here is beyond me. Didn't you see the signs?'

'I was following the ponies.'

'What ponies?' Sue demanded.

'Never mind.' He sighed and then looked out across the deceptively smooth green surface. 'The disaster must have been water. Perhaps they uncovered a giant underground spring or something.'

'Let's get you back to the hotel.' Sue looked more than a little worried. 'You're probably running a fever.'

Tim shook his head.

'Not now,' he said, 'not now.'

SATAN AND A LOAD OF BIBLES

A Mr Henry Llewelyn, having been sent to Samuel Davies, of Ystrad Defodoc Parish in Glamorganshire, to fetch a load of books, viz., Bibles, Testaments, Watts Psalms, Hymns, and Songs for Children, said – Coming home by night towards

Mynyddustwyn, having just passed by Clwyd yr Helygen ale-house, and being in a dry part of the lane – the mare, which he rode, stood still, and, like the ass of the ungodly Balaam, would go no farther, but kept drawing back. Presently he could see a living thing, round like a bowl, rolling from the right hand to the left, and crossing the lane, moving sometimes slow and sometimes very swift – yes, swifter than a bird could fly, though it had neither wings nor feet, – altering also its size. It appeared three times, less one time than another, seemed least when near him, and appeared to roll towards the mare's belly. The mare would then want to go forward, but he stopped her, to see more carefully what manner of thing it was. He stayed, as he thought, about three minutes, to look at it; but, fearing to see a worse sight, he thought it high time to speak to it, and said – 'What seekest thou, thou foul thing? In the name of the Lord Jesus, go away!' And by speaking this it vanished, and sank into the ground near the mare's feet. It appeared to be of a *reddish oak colour.*
From *Welsh Folk-lore* by Rev. Elias Owen, M.A., F.S.A., 1887

MRS JONES

DOROTHY K. HAYNES

I saw Mrs Jones the other day. She looked very much as she always did, with her arms white to the elbows with flour. Busy she was, turning and kneading the dough, and she never stopped, all the time she was talking. Not that she said much. What she did say came out in a quick, scared gabble, as if she thought someone might catch her and cut her off before she was finished.

'Dylis,' she said, talking over her shoulder and hardly moving her mouth, 'get me out of here! They said I could go. They said I could go as soon as I'd finished, but it goes on and on . . .' The hands kneaded, and the dough turned dustily on the slab; and there's frightened I was, because I saw that Mrs Jones was sick and tired, and because nobody but myself had seen her since she disappeared two years ago.

She was going to the sale at the chapel, I remember, with a basketful of Welsh cakes. It was a hot day, and she was going very slowly, with her corns jumping, and her ankles swollen with the heat. I was lying in the long grass as she passed me, and I saw how her haunches went up and down heavily, and the hand carrying the basket sweated; and just beside me she gave a little sigh, and laid the basket carefully on the grass, and lowered herself, heavy and ungraceful, to a big boulder inviting enough for a seat.

Very pathetic she was, sitting there, a fat lady with sore feet, and the Welsh cakes under the white tea towel : but I wasn't quite sure that I liked her. She was a pushing kind of person, always getting herself elected to committees, and always wanting the first place. It was the same with her baking. Every time she entered a competition, she carried off the first prize. I don't know what would have happened if the judges had put her second; and yet there was my sister Gwen, not quite so good at it, but good enough for a bit of encouragement, once in a while; but we're independent, and we wouldn't like people to favour us just because Gwen is not quite the full shilling.

That day, Mrs Jones was entering another competition, before the scones went on to the stall. I could smell them in her basket, and just see them under the towel turned back at one corner. Best Welsh cakes they were, all studded with currants, and round pikelets, bubbly gold and brown, the kind that always put her miles ahead of the other bakers.

There was somebody else besides me showing interest in the basket; a woman, small, only the size of a child. She looked as if she hadn't had a good meal for a week. Her legs were thin, and marled as if they were cold, and her hair hung all straggled on her shoulders. 'Would you have a bite for me to eat, cariad?' she asked, and her fingers moved, as if they would tweak back the towel; but Mrs Jones pulled the basket on to her knees, and said, in that sharp way of hers, 'No, I haven't. They're all for the competition; and I don't bake for the like of you.'

The woman looked at her, and there was a hurt in her face; then the hurt changed to venom, a queer, cruel look, and she nodded her straggly head. 'Well, good luck to you,' she said, 'and I hope you'll be the winner, for we need a good baker. You might have your fill of baking for us yet.'

Mrs Jones said 'Tcha!' and got heaved up again, and waddled off on her corns. What happened to the little woman I don't know. I was too busy thinking I could easily have slipped a hand out and helped myself to a Welsh cake.

Mrs Jones won, of course, and the cakes were sold at twice the price they were worth; and the last anybody saw of her was the Rev. Hughes shaking hands with her as she left. She never reached home; and the police they brought all the way from Tenby found no trace of her for all their questioning.

And then, last week, I saw her. At least, I'm sure I saw her. Everybody asks if I've a witness, but the only one with me was Gwen, and she was too scared to climb up and have a look. And there's scared I was, too, even before I saw Mrs Jones; scared of the rocks, and of the sea, and beginning to worry about the row there would be if mam found out I'd taken Gwen to the Cove. Very dangerous it is, but all right if you understand about the tides; and Gwen, who never gets out much unless I take her, see, had pleaded with me to go down there some time when the tide was low. She's fond of moving water, is Gwen, and we try to keep her away, because they say in time it makes even a sensible person queer.

That day it was Good Friday, and the school had broken up for Easter holidays. Mam was out working, and Gwen and I were all alone in the house; and it was then I remembered that the tide would be low about three o'clock . . . well, it was somewhere to go, a change from the usual old walks I took Gwen, all dressed up after chapel.

There's strange it is, the way the light changes on the Gower coast. The sea was out, far, far away, just a dark line of water turning over and over with a little flash at the edge. On one side of us were the cliffs, with the powdered sand piled round their feet, and on the other side the flat sand, ridged, wrinkled bars of it, and long stretches, wet and bright like a mirror. Gwen was in great spirits at being out. She acts like a child sometimes, as if she was twelve, instead of over twenty. She shook out her hair and pulled off her shoes, and she wanted to run right down to the sea and dance. She said what was the use of all that old space, if she didn't dance in it. But I said there was no time for dancing, and we'd better hurry if we wanted to get to the Cove. Very stern you have to be when Gwen starts her nonsense. Besides, I didn't like the look of the sky. It was too low, and too dark, except where it met the water; and yet the sand was light enough, yellow as the new wood in Mr Thomas's yard.

We hurried along under this lowering sky, with Gwen lagging behind sometimes, and sometimes darting in front, till we came to the edge of the sand, where the cliff runs out to the sea. The tide was coming in a little, but there was a strip of shingle still dry, like white and broken bones; so we crunched round the great layered hang of the cliff, and into the still, lonely place they call Gulls' Cove.

I don't know why we ever went there. From the start, I didn't like it. I'd never been there before, for all we lived so near, and there seemed to be a silence about the place, even though there was more sound than on the sands. The sea, which had been turning and tumbling so far away, came right up now, rolling the white pebbles, and splashing at the lowest rocks, and there was a mewing and whining of seabirds, and the fan of wings in our faces. I stood and listened, and the air seemed dead with silence; and I was giddy with looking up, and seeing the long flat slabs of rock all smeared and crusted with gull droppings.

It wasn't good for Gwen, either. She was acting silly, doing dangerous things, standing beside deep water, and muttering to herself. I felt that we ought to go; and then, high over my head, I thought I heard a voice calling.

'It's only the gulls,' I thought; but the voice was human,

terribly weary and hopeless. Then I thought it might be some boy got hurt looking for birds' eggs, so I looked for a ledge where he might be lying. Sure enough, there was a ledge I could just climb to, if I was careful.

I went up slow and steady, wondering if I was doing right, and trying not to think how far there was to fall. If I hurt myself, and there was only Gwen . . . I got on to the ledge, shaking and scared, and there was nobody there, nothing but a coating of gulls' dirt, and a big crack in the cliff, just wide enough for a hand to go in sideways. I looked in, and there was fat Mrs Jones . . . I can remember exactly how she looked, and the size of the big kitchen place where she was standing, cosy, and yet bleak enough to freeze your blood . . .

She asked me to help her, but I didn't say yes or no. I didn't promise. Gwen could prove that to you, if she'd any sense in her old head, but she's silly, and agrees with whoever speaks last. When I went down to her, all white-faced, and told her about Mrs Jones, she cried, and wanted to get away; and I was nearly crying too, what with the fright of seeing her, and then finding that the tide had come in quicker than we expected. The waves came in with a great booming noise, slapping at the black rocks and racing up every channel, and the gulls swerved above us, deafening us with their screams. You'd have thought the whole wide sea was coming at us, all black and white under the black sky; and we had to wade round the headland, with the current tugging at us, and Gwen howling all the time that she'd tell mam about me.

Well, I owned up to it, and I went to the police about Mrs Jones, and they've been at me ever since, though anyone can see they don't believe me. Only one of them is willing to listen, an old man called MacDonald that came all the way from the Islands on the West of Scotland. They laughed at him, the rest of the police, but he's a big man, and strong, and most of the laughing is done behind his back.

There's strange it is listening to him. He speaks in that slow Highland way, and he believes in fairies. Really; a grown up man! And he blames the fairies for this. The *sidh* he calls them, the silent people; and one of them can meet you in broad daylight, and you'd think it was one of your own kind, except maybe for a queerness you remember after, when you think about it. They'll come and ask you for favours, and if you refuse or offend them, they may have their own back on you! and it's not only in Hell your punishment lasts for ever.

That's what happened to Mrs Jones. They set her to baking, and she can't get free till she's finished; and she never *can* get finished. But there's a way out, if only somebody would tell her. Constable MacDonald says so. All she has to do is to bake up the flour she dusts the board with, the dusting flour scattered all round her. If she does that, she'll finish her task, and they won't be able to keep her. He told me this, and quite a few of the villagers have been to the cove to see if they can't get a glimpse of the fairies' kitchen; but there isn't a cleft or a cave, they say, nothing but a ledge, barely wide enough for a bird to turn on. Certainly a big man like MacDonald couldn't get up there, and I'm beginning to wonder how I managed it. 'You *couldn't* have,' they say; and Gwen's no help, saying first she saw me, and next that she doesn't remember; and would they believe her, anyway, if she sided with me?

'Go on, then,' they say. 'Show us the place. Prove that you can see into it.' The fire brigade are willing to help me with their long ladders and such, and the men from the papers say it'll be worth my while. My mam says it's my duty, and even the Rev. Hughes tries to coax me 'as a gesture of good faith'. But I don't know that I'm keen to have Mrs Jones going about again. There are other women get a chance now she's away. There are no fights at the chapel, no squabbles in the shops, and twice Gwen's had a prize for her baking. There's fine we've managed on our own for the last two years.

Mind you, sorry I was, seeing her standing on her tired feet, with her legs all swollen and aching. She was trying hard, poor soul, trying and trying to get finished. There are times when I cry, thinking about her, and knowing it's me that's keeping her there, but nothing would make me go to the Cove again.

I'm frightened of the rocks, and the big birds, and the water crashing in, and the way the sky lowers over the sea. I'm frightened they might take *me* if I got Mrs Jones away from them. And I couldn't face the poor woman, knowing I was going to refuse her . . .

They can't *make* me go, can they?

THE GHOST OF PONT CNNCA BACH

There are many instances narrated of a ghost's appearance about a bridge called *Pont Cnnca Bach*, near Yscarhir, Carmarthenshire, and it is said that a labourer going very early to work to Bolcwan, met this grim spectre, which so affrighted him, that he walked into a rivulet near, went out of his road through hedges and ditches, in a state of aberration of mind, and as soon as he entered the house fell down in a fit! Another person of the name of Davies, now residing at Carmarthen, returning home about the time

'When the curfew with his sullen note,
Unchainèd to roam the earth each elfin sprite,'

heard a strange rustling noise before he came to this bridge, as if someone was following him, but he did not pay much attention to it until he sat down to rest himself on a field gate, when he heard it distinctly; not being at all daunted, he demanded who was there? when there immediately appeared to his view a grim goblin, who 'grinned horribly a ghastly smile,' and at the sound of his voice

'– shrunk in haste away,
And vanish'd from his sight.'

He can corroborate this, as he has not yet become a member of these *corps terrifique*; and I have been informed by persons who have experienced it, that in crossing this bridge people have been seized with a kind of *cold dread*, similar to that of *Cyoeraeth*, and felt a peculiar sensation which they could not describe.

From *Cambrian Superstitions* by W. Howells, 1831

THE REVEREND JOHN JONES AND THE GHOSTLY HORSEMAN

RONALD SETH

At the beginning of the last century, the Reverend John Jones was minister of Bala, in Merionethshire. He was a clergyman of high principle and unblemished character, and was famed throughout the whole Principality for the zeal and fervour with which he preached the Gospel.

Because of his gift of oratory, he was much in demand at religious meetings, and having appreciated that his eloquence had been bestowed upon him by the Almighty so that he might use it as an instrument to bring souls to salvation, he never refused a request to speak, no matter how far he would have to travel from his own parish. In the summer of 1820 he had received such an invitation to attend a religious meeting at Machynlleth, in the neighbouring country of Montgomery.

He left his house in Bala about two o'clock in the afternoon, travelling on horseback and alone. It was a hot day, and when he reached the village of Llanwchllyn he stopped at the inn to water his horse and refresh himself with a stoup of ale. As he sat on the bench outside the inn, tasting his ale and watching his beast drink deeply at the trough, he noticed a man reclining in the shade of a tree. By the man's side was a sickle sheathed in straw, and from this, and from the man's appearance, Mr Jones judged that he was an itinerant reaper in search of employment.

When the minister had finished his ale, he put down the mug on the bench beside him, and took from his pocket his heavy silver watch, flicked open the front and saw that if he were to reach Machynlleth in time he must delay no longer. As he put his watch back into his pocket he happened to glance across at the man, and saw that he was now sitting up and was watching him.

Mr Jones remounted his horse, and set off. The next part of his journey lay through a wild and desolate region, almost completely uninhabited.

When he had ridden for about an hour, and was on the point of emerging from a wood at the top of a long and steep slope, he saw a man coming towards him on foot. As the man drew nearer, Mr Jones recognised him as the man who had been resting near the inn in Llanwchllyn. On coming up, the man touched his hat, and said, 'Good day to you, Minister, is it possible that you can tell me what hour it is?'

'Why certainly,' the parson replied, feeling in his pocket for his watch. 'It is a few minutes past a quarter after four.'

'I am obliged to you, sir,' the man said, touching his hat again. 'Good journey to you.'

'And good day to you, my good man,' replied Mr Jones, and urged his horse on once more.

The track down the hill was bordered on both sides by tall hedgerows, and at the foot of the hill was a gate which gave access to a field through which the next part of the track ran. When he was about half-way down the hill, Jones's attention was attracted by something moving on the other side of the hedge on his left, and going in the same direction as himself.

At first he thought it must be an animal of one kind or another, but when he came to a place in the hedge where the bushes were lower than the rest and not so thick, he saw that it was a man bent double and that over his shoulder he carried a sickle sheathed in straw.

Made curious by the man's strange behaviour, the parson watched him for some time wondering what he could be about. But when he saw the man stop, kneel on one knee and begin to unsheathe his sickle, he felt a shudder of fear pass through him. For he recalled that the man had seen his watch, which was a valuable one, and now seemed to be preparing to attack him as he reached the gate, in order to rob him of it, since while Jones watched, he had run on to the gate and was crouched down behind a bush beside it.

Though he was at this time in his early thirties, and was sturdy and strong, the minister was totally unarmed, and would be at a grave disadvantage in warding off any attack from a man armed with a sharp sickle. He reined in his horse, and looked about him in all directions, hoping to see someone he could tell his fears to and for whose help he might plead. But there was not a person in sight.

His fear mounting as each minute passed, he considered that discretion would be the better part of valour, and had actually half-turned his horse, intending to make his way home again, when he realized that his craven alarm was about to make him temporarily forsake the Lord. What he was doing, and from the same motives, was what Peter had done when he had denied Jesus thrice before cock-crow.

The meeting which he was on his way to attend was a very important one. Many would attend it seeking the Lord, and he had been asked especially to speak to them so that his inspired words might show them the way. If he did not go, he told himself, how many might be lost that day who but for his cowardice would have been saved. As long as there existed the faintest possibility of his getting there, he must go on.

Right though this decision might be, however, it did not change the situation in which he found himself. Only a few hundred yards away from him was an armed man waiting to spring on him while he was at a disadvantage. For in order to continue he must pause at the gate, open it, pass through and close it behind him.

What could he do to make the attack fail? Should he put his heels to his horse, urge her at the gate, hoping that she would leap over it? But she was aged and docile, and in the four or five years that he had owned her she had never once been put into a gallop, and certainly had never leapt over anything, let alone a five-barred gate. If only the gate had been open!

He then looked about him, wondering whether he could leave the track and make his way across the fields. But this was not possible either. Where the hedges were not too high, they were too thick with brambles for the horse to pass through; and even where, on his right, there were open gaps in the hedges, these gaps were protected by sheer rocky banks which only a beast far more nimble than his mount could hope to negotiate with success.

He could not go back, and ever again be at peace with his conscience; an alternative route was denied him; and to go forward he must risk a personal encounter with his potential armed assailant, the outcome of which, unless a miracle happened, must certainly mean his injury, if not his death.

Once again he pulled himself together. For a minister of God he was exhibiting an unforgivable lack of trust and confidence in Divine protection.

'I am a weak and sinful man, O Lord!' he groaned. 'Please show me what I must do!'

For several moments he bowed his head in silent prayer. As he confessed later: 'For all my self-abasement, I prayed rather in despair than in a spirit of humble trust and confidence. Yet, when I had said my Amen, my prayers seemed to have had a soothing effect on my mind, so that, refreshed and invigorated, I proceeded anew to consider the difficulties of my position.'

Aged and slow though his mare might be, by this time she had grown impatient at the delay, and of her own accord began to move off down the slope. Jones had allowed the reins to fall on her neck while he had been pondering what to do, and her unexpected movement made him clutch at them. He pulled on them to check her, but as he did so his eyes fell upon an object close to him, and he saw to his utter astonishment that he was no longer alone.

There by his side was another horseman. He was dressed in a black suit and hat, which contrasted sharply with the whiteness of his mount. Jones's surprise at seeing him there was so intense that for several moments he was unable to speak.

'He had appeared,' the minister recounted, 'as suddenly as if he had sprung from the earth. He must have been riding behind me and overtaken me. And yet I had not heard the slightest sound. It was mysterious and inexplicable!'

Now his situation was completely changed, for no assailant, however desperate, would attempt to attack two opponents. Overjoyed by his release from his perilous position, Jones soon overcame his feelings of wonder, and he began to speak to his companion.

'Have you seen a man since you came out of the wood?' he asked.

Having waited for some seconds for an answer and not receiving one, he went on: 'Hiding down there by the gate is a man with a sickle. He has designs upon my silver watch, and possibly upon the few coins I have on me. Did you see him?'

Still the man did not reply, and becoming embarrassed the minister said: 'I cannot tell you how happy your coming has made me. I have desperately been considering what to do. I am on my way to Machynlleth to address an evangelist meeting there. I had thought of turning back, may the good God forgive me, but then I thought of the souls I might save from damnation with my humble words, and knew I must go on. But I could see no way of avoiding an encounter with the villain yonder. Now that you have come, I have no longer any fear. Shall we go on?'

He turned and looked at his companion, and realised that the man had been giving him only the slightest attention, but was gazing intently in the direction of the gate at the bottom of the hill. His embarrassment increased, particularly as the horseman seemed deliberately disdaining to reply to him. So he decided to keep his peace, and looked in the direction of the gate.

And now he received yet another surprise. For as he watched he saw the reaper come out of his hiding place and begin to run across the field to the left, re-sheathing his sickle as he went.

'There he goes!' he pointed excitedly. 'Perhaps you thought I had been imagining the man. But now you can see him.'

His companion nodded, but still did not speak.

Almost overwhelmed with relief at the passing of the danger, Jones urged his mare forward, and the horseman rode by his side towards the gate. The relief had made the minister even more garrulous, and as they went he continued to address the man in black, though he was both surprised and not a little hurt by the traveller's continued and, as it seemed to him, mysterious silence.

As they reached the gate the figure of the reaper was disappearing over the brow of a neighbouring hill.

'He has gone!' the minister sighed. Then to the horseman, 'Can it be doubted for a moment that my prayer for help was heard, and that you were sent for my deliverance by the Lord!'

It was at this point that the minister realised that, having from his appearance judged the horseman to be English, he had spoken in the English tongue ever since he had been in his company. He is a Welshman, he told himself, who does not or will not speak English, and he repeated his last question in Welsh.

To his joy the man at once replied, with a single word, *Amen*.

As he rode forward to examine the fastening of the gate, Jones continued to ply his companion with questions in the Welsh.

'Have you come far, sir? Are you going far? I am going to a religious gathering at Machynlleth; are you going in that direction? If you are, perhaps you will give me the honour and extreme pleasure of your company? Or is your destination Llangollen; or are you perhaps going south? It is deserted countryside hereabouts . . .'

While he was speaking, he was pulling at the latch of the gate with his stick. It was proving a difficult operation, and for a moment he thought he would have to dismount; but at last the latch came up and the gate swung slowly into the field.

Jones pulled his horse to one side, and as he turned towards where he expected to find a horseman waiting he said, 'Do you go on . . .'

He did not finish the sentence, for the horseman had disappeared.

Dumbfounded, the minister looked up the slope, the whole of which he could see. The horseman was not in sight, and yet if he had returned by the way he had come he could not have had time to reach the wood.

'What could have become of him?' I asked myself, the minister recorded in an account of his experiences which were later included in a memoir published in a number of the Welsh quarterly periodical *The Essayist*, in commemoration of his recent death in 1853. 'He could not have gone through the gate, nor have made his horse leap the high hedges which on both sides shut in the road.

'Where was he? Had I been dreaming? Was it an apparition, a spectre which had been riding by my side for the last ten minutes? Could it be possible that I had seen no man or horse at all, and that the vision was but a creature of my imagination?

'I tried hard to convince myself that this was the case, but in vain; for unless someone had been with me, why had the reaper re-sheathed his murderous-looking weapon and fled? Surely, no; this mysterious horseman was no creation of my brain. I had seen him; who could he have been?

'I asked myself this question again and again; and then a feeling of profound awe began to creep over my soul. I remembered the singular way of his first appearance – his long silence – and then again the single word to which he had given utterance; I called to mind that this reply had been elicited from him by my mentioning in our own tongue the name of the Lord, and that this was the single occasion on which I had done so.

'What could I then believe? – but one thing, and that was that my prayer had indeed been heard, and that help had been given me from on high at a time of great danger.

'Full of this thought I dismounted, and throwing myself on my knees I offered up a prayer of thankfulness to Him who had heard my cry, and found help for me in time of need.

'I then mounted my horse and continued my journey. But

through the long years that have elapsed since that memorable summer's day I have never for a moment wavered in my belief that in the mysterious horseman I had a special interference of Providence, by which means I was delivered from a position of extreme danger.'

CORPSE CANDLES

Every nation has its peculiar superstitions, and as regards the Corpse Candles or, in Welsh, *Cannyllau cyrth*, they are universally known to be endemic (if I may use the expression) to Wales. It appears that these lights are generally observed to veer their course towards the churchyard, which they *enter*, hover round the spot where the person whose death they intimate will be buried, and disappear; they vary in brilliancy and size, according to the person whose doom it is to leave the world; thus an infant's would not be larger than that of a candle, whilst a child's 'of the larger growth' is of a proportionate size; the colour is said to be a sulphurous blue, and when any one observes their approach, if they do not move aside they will be struck down by their force, as I was informed by a person living, whose father coming in contact with one, was thrown off his horse. If they are seen to stop, the corpse will do the same at the funeral; if they move aside, it will occur so at the burial; and should two candles meet, the two funerals will do the same: it is also said that if a person looks back at one after it has passed him, he will perceive the corpse and its attendants.

From *Cambrian Superstitions* by W. Howells, 1831

CADI HUGHES

GLYN JONES

Upstairs in number one Colliers' Row, Ifan Cariad was dying by inches. People often say 'dying by inches' without really meaning it, but as a description of Ifan it was almost literally true; because his left leg was gangrenous to the knee and every day for the last week when Cadi his wife went upstairs to dress it and clean it out she found a new hole, sometimes the size of the palm of her hand, in a different part of his leg or the flesh of his foot. Then yesterday two of his toes had come off into her apron. The disease had started as a small piece of bad skin under the ball of the big toe, and it would soon pass upwards over the knee into his thigh; and then, when his whole leg had become putrid, it would separate from the rest of his body at the hip and lie discarded in the bed beside him. But Ifan would probably be dead before then, poor chap, unless a miracle happened.

Most of the time he was lying sog after the dope the doctor was giving him daily to ease his pain. His face in a short time had become yellow as clay and tiny, hardly bigger than a hand, with his nose rising up tight in the middle like a plucked fowl's breastbone. They had cut his hair short for comfort, and it looked like the pile on black velvet or plush, and fitted like a cap on top of his little monkey-face. And he had become so thin that his body lifted up the bedclothes hardly at all. He never was very much but he had shrunk to nothing. For days he hadn't eaten a bite, and all that had passed his lips was the water that Cadi fed him with out of the spout of the teapot. The smell of cooking nearly made his inside jump out of his belly, but one day near the end he whispered, 'Cadi, give me something to eat.'

'Of course, little Ifan,' she said, humouring him, 'what will you have?'

'I'd like some of that dinner I can smell cooking.'

'Oh, you can't have that, little Ifan,' she said, 'that's the ham boiling for the funeral.'

She was like that, always planning and scheming. She did everything possible for him; it suited her. She wouldn't let the district nurse come near, and when she wasn't actually fussing round him she would pray, or sing hymns in the voice she used when there were strangers in the chapel; not the nice modern hymns about Jesus and harps and rest beyond Jordan, but savage old-time stanzas by cracked Welsh poets preoccupied with punishment and corruption. She was wonderful the way she waited on him. But she had nearly killed him with her bossiness during the twenty years of their married life. When Ifan married her she was worth looking at; she wasn't just pretty like so many of the dark little women with heavy bottoms living in the mining villages, she was a beauty, big and straight, with blue eyes and hair the colour of a new penny. Ifan himself was small and dark; he looked wicked, a handful for any boss, the sort that always smells foul air in the pit and sees too much water in the workings quicker than anybody else, and makes trouble among the men generally. He was all there; and he knew the Mabinogion backwards.

As for her, she had no idea of her own beauty. All she wanted was for things to go on smoothly as she planned them. Anything odd, strange, eccentric, she hated like poison. And Ifan was a bit odd, what with his politics and his vegetarianism. He was a hot socialist but if he went on the stump she held herself off from him and gave him hell. And she didn't just stop with her tongue either. Poor Ifan wasn't much of an agitator in his own house; he had to draw his horns in at number one Colliers' Row or he could look out. She was a holy terror, bossing everybody and making arrangements all round, and turning out such a fuss-arse, and so trivial. And yet Ifan couldn't do without her; he was always a bit soft on her, imagining her, because of her hair, like Rhiannon or Blodeuwedd, or goodness knows who. And he could always think with pleasure of their courting days when the village boys going about in groups used to sing after the courting couples strolling up towards the lonelier roads:

Red are the shivvies and red are the hips,
  Hazel nuts are brown;
Two of us climb up the Pandy tips
  And three of us come down.
Hoo!

There were more verses.

It was then he got his nickname. He was really Ifan Hughes, although everybody called him Ifan Cariad, which signifies Ifan the Lover, or Ifan the Sweetheart. He used to tap at the window of her house at night when he was calling for her, and her mother would call out from inside, 'Who is there?'

'Ifan,' he would answer.

'Which Ifan?'

'Ifan the lover of Cadi.'

The neighbours heard, and such a chance for a nickname seemed like a godsend. He became known as Ifan Cariad Cadi, Ifan the lover of Cadi, or Ifan Cariad. But such a name in the village was never taken as a sign of disrespect. Everybody else had a nickname anyway.

Sunday morning, just as it was getting light, Cadi came into the bedroom to see if he was still alive. It was a bitter raw morning with no sun and thick clouds *crêped* like slab rubber over the sky. He was all right, but just as she was going back to bed someone started knocking hard at the front door. Cadi was surprised, it was so early. She leaned over the banister and saw someone standing outside the figured glass panel she had had put in the middle of the door to best her sister-in-law. It was just a big dark shape, she couldn't tell who, although she stood there guessing instead of going to see. She slipped a petticoat over her head and got into a jacket of Ifan's, shouting, 'Who's there?' There was no answer but the knocking started again, louder this time as though it wasn't going to stop in a hurry.

She opened the door.

It was God.

He was tall, dressed in a dirty green tweed suit with patch pockets and leather buttons but not much better than rags. There was a sack pinned round his shoulders, and on his head was a cloth slouch hat with the brim turned down over his eyes. His clothes were so disreputable, and yet he looked big and splendid somehow. His left leg finished at the knee, and he hugged a rough wooden crutch as thick as a bedpost, with some of the bark still on it, not padded at all, and spreading out like petals at the end. His grey beard was long but rather thin, and much of his skin was covered with red blind boils like rivet heads. His face was handsome though; patriarchal and majestic, but a bit seedy, and his hair was on his collar. She knew him all right.

'Let me in, Cadi,' he said. He was her boss.

She did so, and upstairs he went sprightly enough, and straight into Ifan's room. There was chaff on his back and horse-dung on the heel of his boot.

'What do you want with us, little God?' she asked upstairs, rather anxious. He and Ifan were smiling at one another, knowingly, as though they had something good up their sleeve.

'I've come for Ifan,' he said, still smiling and hardly looking at her.

Although she half expected it, it was a good bit of a shock to hear him say it straight out like that. 'O little God,' she began, sobbing, 'don't take Ifan; I can't live with my brother, his wife quarrels with me, and I'm too respectable to be a washer-woman or go to the Big House.'

Ifan grinned. He was a bit pinker than he had been, and more arrogant already.

'I must take him all the same,' said God.

He stood his crutch against the commode and sat on the edge of the bed, quite at home, like a preacher. His eyes were cunning and very bright, with the skin drawn in all around as though his visit were a bit of a lark. He took very little notice of Cadi except to glance at her sometimes with his spotted eyes. She had more or less gone to pieces; all her bossiness and importance had got flat. She snivelled and started to whimper again.

'Take my daughter, Esther Cariad,' she moaned, 'she's unemployed and hard for us to keep.'

'A cup of tea before we go, please,' said God. 'No fear,' he continued, 'it's not I'll be coming for her, Cadi.'

Ifan nodded and looked serious.

She hung about whimpering for a bit and then went downstairs almost gladly to make the tea, and when she returned Ifan was sitting on the side of the bed dressing, with his huge bandaged leg hanging over the edge. She set the tray down hurriedly and started off on another tack. 'Little Ifan,' she pleaded, going up to him, 'don't go and leave me, and me so good to you always.'

Ifan looked at God, one leg in his trousers.

'Not so good, Cadi,' he said, putting his saucer down.

'Indeed I have, little God,' she answered reddening, 'you don't know. I've nursed him hand and foot in illnesses and accidents, and pinched myself in the strikes for him and Esther.'

'Ay I know,' he said, 'but what about having the bile on Labour Day, and throwing his Cheap Editions on the fire, and hiding the pennies for the gas so that he couldn't read at night, and keeping him home from his meetings to do the garden? You're a bitch, Cadi.'

She smiled hoping to humour him. 'It was only a bit of fun,' she said; and seeing Ifan in difficulties over some vital buttons she was bound to go and help him.

'Very humorous,' said God. 'Anyway, come on, Ifan, get on my back. Cadi, thank you for the nice tea. We must be shifting.'

She could see they were going in good earnest. She was red and serious again and desperate. 'Don't go,' she cried. 'Ifan, stop. Let me get you a clean nightshirt first, then.'

'Lay off,' said God, 'you'll tip us.'

'Plenty of nightshirts where I'm going,' said Ifan grinning. 'Good-bye, Cadi.'

Downstairs they went, not too badly. When they were in the passage, seeing them going for good and all, Cadi shouted down over the banister, 'Ifan, have you got a clean handkerchief?'

God put him down quickly in the oak chair Cadi had in the passage for fashion and came headlong back upstairs. He swung at her with his crutch and hit her into the corner by the chest-of-drawers. She lay there in a heap without a sound, her mop of hair half down and her false teeth hanging out of her mouth.

God and Ifan hurried out of the house as fast as they could go, shutting the glass panelled door with a bang behind them.

THE WHITE LADY OF ABERGLASLYN PASS

'The White Lady of the Pass' is an object of great attraction to all tourists. It is a white stone forming a sharp projection in the rock above the river, at a height of some three hundred feet. It is best seen from the point at which it first comes to view, in approaching the Pass from Bedd Gelert. We saw it for the first time on a bright moonlight night one September, and the optical delusion was perfect. Few people would ever imagine that this stone is the fossilised form of a real lady, and the reader may, in his impatience, use strong terms at our folly in mentioning it; but, alas! has she not haunted this Pass for years, and caused so many fatal frights that the things cannot be stated in terms of discussion? We know not what strange story lies buried in the past, telling how she met her fearful fate. She nearly always appeared to a person about to meet with a serious accident or a sudden death. Her ghostly doings were at last arrested, and she was fossilised, and made the gazing stock of all men.

She was, however, not the last ghost that has been seen in the Pass. A man still living has told us the story of his own adventure while returning from the village late at night, on his way home to Portmadoc. He was walking along at a steady pace, thinking of the sweetheart whom he had newly left, when a huge mastiff, the size of a year-old calf, walked up beside him, from he knows not where. He trembled like a leaf, and paused to gaze at the creature, while a cold perspiration trickled down his face. While he was considering what to do, the mastiff vanished, and was not seen by him again. The late David Evans, Meillionen, twice met a ghost in this place; once it appeared to him as a figure of fire. He was both times on horseback, and, the last time, he and the horse took such fright that both suffered in consequence. His life was, for a time, almost despaired of. The late Rev. William Ellis, Bedd Gelert, insisted until his dying day that he also had seen something in the Pass, of which he could give no account, though the recalling of it always gave him a cold shudder.

From *Bedd Gelert, its Fact, Fairies, and Folk-lore,*

by D. E. Jenkins

BLACK GODDESS

JACK GRIFFITH

Bill Rees was mad!

Iestyn Morgan had suspected it for a long time; now he was sure of it.

It was autumn 1930, and they were sitting in an underground lodge of a coal mine, eating their food. The lodge was simply a hole left behind in the workings as the coal face had advanced. It was barely large enough to hold both of them as they sat side by side on a sleeper converted into a seat.

They were discussing mutual problems for running their

district where Bill was fireman, the official in charge, and Iestyn his assistant.

Bill looked out of place in a mine, with his sensitive face and beautiful features. And his soul seemed to be beating at powerful but invisible barriers which denied it freedom where it could exist unfettered and without restraint.

He worked in the mines because it was a job into which circumstances had forced him. Yet, although he hated everything associated with it, he had become a minor official.

Iestyn was different. He was strong in body and solid in mind. Although some years younger than Bill he was already a qualified colliery manager, for mining was his chosen career as it had been his father's. Being a junior official was just a period of preparation for more important things.

Even their eating was different. Bill consumed delicate little sandwiches with care, throwing away the corners marked by dusty fingers. Iestyn gobbled bread-and-butter and a tomato he dipped into salt in a screwed-up piece of paper. He ate everything, dust and all.

Yet they were fond of each other, and Iestyn was concerned at Bill's condition even though he felt there was nothing he could do about it.

When they had finished their food they also stopped talking. Iestyn leaned his head back and dozed. Bill's chin rested on his hands, his elbows on his knees. Everything was silent and still.

Iestyn stirred uncomfortably, his body cramped. He lifted his head, suddenly becoming alert. The expression on Bill's face, lit by a lamp a few inches away, disturbed him.

'Feeling O.K., Bill?' he asked.

Bill turned his head, his blue eyes showing distant paleness. 'Yes. Why?' His voice, too, seemed distant.

'Oh – nothing, only you look thoughtful.'

They did not speak again for a while. Once more Iestyn dozed.

Suddenly Bill broke the silence. 'Tell me, Iestyn, have you ever noticed anything peculiar in the pit?'

Iestyn grinned and tried to scrape an unpleasant taste from

his tongue. 'Everything from the manager down,' he replied.

'I didn't mean that. I meant something queer.'

Iestyn's grin vanished. From the privacy of the gloom he peered at his companion's face. 'What do you mean, queer?' he asked, attempting to sound casual.

Bill looked at him and cried, 'Haven't you ever felt that there's something queer in the pit? Some evil influence spreading itself everywhere, trying to capture the souls of men and destroy them before it kills their bodies?'

Iestyn stiffened. This was it! He swallowed, but there was nothing to swallow. 'Can't say I have,' he murmured. 'Why, have *you*?'

'Often! I can see it grinning at me as if it's about to pounce. I'm afraid of it, only I won't let it see that I am. Once it knows I'm afraid of it, it will get me. It'll kill me, and I don't want to be killed. I don't want to die – here – down in the pit. I want to die somewhere else where my spirit can be free, not imprisoned in this hole for ever. If I die here, Iestyn, I'll never get away; I'll be a prisoner here for all eternity.'

Iestyn tried to reassure him. 'You're not going to die, Bill. Don't be a fool and start thinking things like that.'

He wanted to say more, but did not know what. He wondered whether madmen really were endowed with superhuman strength as they were reputed to be.

'It wants to kill me,' Bill went on tragically. 'And I don't want to die. It killed George last week, and Ianto Twp is in hospital with his spine smashed. He's going to die; the spirit got him. I tell you –'

'Don't you worry about Ianto; he took his chance like the rest of us. And you won't have to stick this job all your life, either: you'll get one outside some day, and forget all about it.'

'Forget all about it!' Bill's voice was shrill and trembling. Had there been room he would have risen from his seat. 'D'you think I can forget about this – this spirit of evil demanding human sacrifices – even burnt offerings – to satisfy its cruel appetites? *Thou shall have no other gods before me, for I, the*

Lord thy god, am a jealous god. All cruel gods are the same, cruel and jealous. It's a Black God, Iestyn, a Black God that rules everything in the pit. It's a cruel god, cruel, cruel cruel . . .'

His voice trailed away. He pressed his face into his hands.

Iestyn knew for certain that Bill was mad, yet did not know what to do about it. He ought to report it at the end of the shift, even though Bill would be sacked, perhaps even put away. Yet – against what he knew to be true – he hoped it might be only a state of temporary depression. Tomorrow, and he would be all right . . .

Although it was long past their usual time for returning to work Iestyn was afraid of letting Bill get away from him. He wanted to see him in a more normal condition first.

'A Black God,' he said suddenly, trying to find something to talk about and delay their leaving. 'You must mean a Black Goddess. If it's cruel and callous it's probably a female. The female is the cruel one. "The female of the species . . ." '

Bill looked up sharply. 'A Black Goddess!' His voice was quiet and clear. 'That's it: a Black Goddess.' Then his voice lost its vigour. 'No, it's got a big face, like a giant, a Russian giant with a big beard. He's got a robe on, and a belt round his waist. And he's always laughing; only you can't hear him, you can only see him.' He took his cap off and ran his fingers through his long hair. 'You can't hear him; you just know he's doing it.'

Iestyn tapped the crumbs out of his food box and put the lid on, then pushed the box into his pocket. 'Then there's only one thing to do: laugh back at it; laugh back at it like hell,' he said. 'Well, boy, much as I hate to say it, it's time we went. The whole district might be on stop for all we know.'

He squeezed his way out to the main roadway and took off his jacket. He hung it on a nail in the lodge.

Bill remained sitting, gazing at the gloom of the heading where Iestyn was, his face grave with concern. 'Perhaps you're right,' he murmured; 'it might have been a woman after all. A witch. An old witch trying to be big but succeeding only in being cruel. A shabby black witch trying to be a Black Goddess.'

Iestyn did not know what to do. If Bill went on talking and thinking like this anything could happen. He had known Bill for so long that it was difficult to realise that he was different from what he had always been. But today he was quite mad. What had been suspicion was now understanding. But what could he do? Interest in work might delay anything unpleasant until the end of the shift, so he must get him back to work. 'Come on,' he cried; 'let's put a jerk in it. We'll never finish our rounds if we don't put a move on.'

A sound of footsteps came from around the bend where one road went off to the right, dividing the district into two. Beams of light followed it.

'Put a jerk in it, Bill,' Iestyn whispered. 'There's someone coming round the turn from Enoch's.'

Bill scrambled out of the lodge, pulling off his jacket and hanging his lamp on his belt.

A man came dimly into sight where the roads joined.

'Hoi,' Iestyn called.

'Where's Bill?' the newcomer asked.

'Oh, it's you, Dick,' Bill replied. 'Here I am. What do you want?'

'There's a hell of a fall on D.7. conveyor. It's all on stop. The whole place is blocked up; I think the whole place have fell in.'

'Good God! It was all right this morning.'

'Aye, it's only been on work about a half-hour.'

'Come on,' Bill cried, leading the way towards the conveyor.

'Come on, Dick,' Iestyn called, following him.

The conveyor was a metal trough which jerked coal along to fall eventually into trams waiting at one end. It was about eighty yards long.

The three men hurried towards the road at the other end.

Bill squeezed past a horse attached to an empty tram just inside the mouth of the road. The tram had gone off the rails, a corner getting jammed against a post supporting the side.

'Give us a shove on the fourpenny side, Morgans,' the haulier called to Iestyn as the latter scrambled past.

'It's an empty,' came the retort. 'Why don't you shove it on yourself?'

'It's a bad dram, mun,' the haulier explained. 'The wheel's all loose. Give us a lift on the front end and I'll be able to shove it on the rail on my own.'

But Iestyn was gone. 'Dick'll give you a lift,' he called.

When Dick arrived the haulier said, 'He's jammed fast as hell. Get on in front and let's shove him back.'

They put their buttocks against the tram and heaved.

'Stamback,' the haulier called to the horse who moved gingerly against the metal shafts. 'Stamback. Stamback-stambackstambackstamback.' Nothing happened.

Dick stopped pushing. 'Nothing doing, Shoni,' he said. 'Horses are no good at backing underground.'

'We've got to get the damn thing loose somehow,' Shoni muttered, turning to examine the place where the tram was stuck against the post. 'We'll have to try and pull it forward.'

Dick turned the beam of his lamp towards the roof. 'You'll pull a hell of a fall if you ent careful,' he warned.

'I'll pull the lousy pit in for tuppence,' Shoni muttered. 'Get out of the way a bit.'

Dick did so.

Shoni turned to the horse and cried, 'Now then, my flower: come up, come up.'

The horse gave a sharp tug but stopped when it felt strong resistance.

'Come up, come up. Duke, come up; come up.'

Duke responded with all he had. His stomach almost scraped the ground; his blood vessels stood out like whips.

Suddenly the tram came loose, tearing a huge scar along the post. It rumbled forward, rising and falling over sleepers and rough ground. Shoni sprang on to the iron 'gun' which connected the shafts to the tram.

'Steady, old china,' he shouted. 'Whoa, my flower.'

He ducked as they passed under a collar, a cross-piece lower than the rest. The tram struck the side and bounced across the road. It caught a post, broken but not completely severed, and knocked it out. The collar collapsed under a shower of dirt and stones. The tram jammed again, the horse plunging and struggling to go forward. Shoni, dazed by a falling stone, tried to get past.

Then the roof came down – massive, thundering – behind him.

Something falling struck him. He staggered and fell on his face.

'His foot's on my neck,' he mumbled. 'His foot's on my neck . . .'

The fall, still sounding like thunder, increased to immensity as Dick dragged the now unconscious Shoni to a safer place.

Bill and Iestyn paused when they heard the crash, then turned and hurried back, followed by John Daniel, a member of one of the more rigid religious denominations, and a fifteen-year-old boy named Tommy. They worked at the nearer end of the conveyor, next to Dick.

Iestyn examined Shoni while, with Tommy's electric lamp, Bill and Dick approached the fall. Thick dust was settling again, the dimmed lights becoming less obscure. Grim, puritanical John Daniel remained standing, his arms folded across his black and hairy chest draped with a torn singlet. Tommy stood near Iestyn, uncertain of what was happening. He had been working underground only a few months, and was not used to it. His face was like a cherub's, and an old cap of his father's would have made him look comic had it not been pathetic. He was nervous and wished Dick would come to him.

Soon they were able to observe the size of the fall. It was like a mountain of boulders sprinkled with protruding props of timber near the base. The tram was buried almost completely. Iestyn, followed by Tommy, joined Bill and Dick.

'Duw,' Iestyn muttered, stooping and peering up under an overhanging rock.

'How we going to get out, Dick?' Tommy's querulous treble startled the others.

The men glanced at each other. They hadn't thought about it.

Dick spat into the dust, then said, 'We'll have it cleared away in no time, bach. Only they'll have to do it from the other side, so we might be a bit late going out tonight.'

'But why can't we shift it from this side?'

''Cos . . . 'cos . . . 'cos we ent got nowhere to put the muck when we shift it, see; that's why.'

'Aye, that's it,' Iestyn agreed. 'You go back and sit down, Tommy, and have a rest.'

'Aye,' Dick said brightly, taking the boy's arm and leading him away, 'you come back and sit by Shoni. You look after him and – and watch the beetles don't crawl over him.' He lowered his voice. 'And have a sleep if you can. The bosses won't say nothing at a time like this.'

Although they did not say so the men knew they were entombed, trapped between two falls. They sweated. The air was hot, for ventilation had been checked if not actually stopped. For a while they peeped and scouted vainly for a way of escape, then stood in moody silence. After a while Iestyn went back from the fall and sat on a pile of timber. The others also sat down.

'Put those electric lamps out,' Iestyn advised. 'We'll be glad of all the light we can get later on. God knows how long we'll be down here.'

Bill looked at him, a hunted expression on his face. He had spoken little, which made Iestyn afraid he was thinking too much.

The others switched off their lights. Only Bill's oil-lamp remained burning. The flame was topped with transparent blue, like a small gas-cap. Tiny golden specks sped up it to oblivion.

Iestyn slid off the timber and lay on the floor.

'It's getting hot as hell,' Dick muttered, removing a sharp stone from under his shoulder.

'Of course it's getting hot,' John Daniel agreed grimly.

'There's no air coming in, is there?'

Bill's face had been in his hands; he looked up. 'No air!' he cried. 'No air! We must have air or we'll die!'

'Shut up, you bloody fool; you'll frighten the kid,' said Dick in a low voice. Then, louder, 'You all right, there, Tommy?'

'Aye, I'm all right, Dick. And Shoni is saying something now.'

Iestyn went to him. Shoni was muttering, 'His foot's on my neck; his foot's on my neck.' He sat up, rubbing the back of his head. He gazed at Iestyn's dim form silhouetted against the feeble lamplight. 'I felt his foot coming right down on my neck. Knocked me sick, aye.'

Iestyn told him it was a stone, not the horse's hoof which had struck him. But Shoni insisted, 'I know it was his foot. I could feel his tip.'

'Come over here, Tommy bach,' Dick invited, raising a black and shining arm. 'Lie down by here and have a sleep. You'll be all right.' The boy snuggled under it gratefully.

Shoni, still rubbing his head, went to the edge of the fall. 'Tidy little hayrick,' he said, viewing the mass of earth and stones. Sweat ran down into his eyes, burning them. He saw that the stones were damp with condensation. 'Duw, Duw, even the stones are sweating.' He turned sharply, screwing the pot of his lamp to light it. 'Where's Duke? Is he all right?'

'He's O.K.,' Iestyn replied. 'He's on inside.'

Shoni stumbled through the gloom towards the shadowy figure of the horse. With lamp lifted he examined the animal's back. There was a long, deep scratch across the haunches. Shoni wiped it with the hem of a football jersey he wore instead of a shirt.

'I'll wash it clean for you, butty,' he muttered affectionately.

Taking a water-jack from the side of the road, he was about to pour water over the cut when Iestyn saw what he was doing.

'Don't waste that water, you flaming lunatic,' the latter cried. 'We'll want all we can get of that. God knows when we're going to get out of here.'

'Sorry, Morgans.' The haulier replaced the cork. Then, to the horse, 'We'll have to do it when we get out tonight, bach.' He sat down again.

The others slept or dozed. Shoni, who lay asleep across the tram-rails, snored so loudly that he kept waking up. Duke shook himself until his harness jingled.

For a while nothing could be heard except heavy breathing, the rattle of Duke's harness and the shuffle of his hoofs, and the occasional hollow thud of a 'pounce' in the coal-face.

Iestyn stirred, moving his body which had become cramped. His head ached and his chest felt compressed. He sighed as if in pain. Tommy, sweating under Dick's arm, moaned softly. He was hot and uncomfortable, but affection for Dick kept him close. He sat up and tried to spit, but the saliva clung stickily to his lips and fell over his chin. He wiped it with a damp, black arm.

Bill was the only one really awake. He had been thinking continuously, while the others had been idly ruminating until they had fallen asleep. He picked up his lamp; the glass had become smoked and brown. He held it by the heavy brass pot and blew through the ventilation holes at the top. The flame brightened. He blew again, rotating the lamp so that he could clear the many holes in turn. Then he put it down again, holding it by the handle.

As it was lowered it revolved slightly, and a splash of mud which had been on the glass all day flung a shadow which turned as the lamp turned. Bill yelled, dropping the lamp. It went out.

The others scrambled to their feet, switching their lights on.

''s matter?' Shoni asked, dazed from sleep.

'What the hell's the matter with you, Bill?' Iestyn cried, half afraid of finding out.

'I saw it!' Bill shrieked, pointing a finger. 'I saw it! I saw it again!'

'Saw what?'

'That black thing! That Black Goddess! She's trying to kill me all the time.'

Iestyn pushed his dusty cap back from his forehead and rubbed his chin. 'Everything's all right boys; it's something between Bill and me,' he tried to assure the others. 'Don't you worry; I know what it is.'

'It's I who know what it is,' Bill cried, his voice tense with passion. 'It's something that's trying to kill me. It's trying to kill us all. Give me that lamp.' He grabbed Iestyn's.

Iestyn clung to it. 'What do you want it for?'

'I'm going to get out of here – now – and I want a lamp to see with. Give it to me, I tell you.'

'All right; all right.' Iestyn's voice was soothing. 'But how are you going to manage to get out? I want to come with you, that's all; I don't want to stop down here longer than I can help.'

Silently the others watched. They could not understand but they realised that something odd was happening.

'How are you going to get out?' Iestyn repeated, still clinging to the lamp.

Bill's eyes puckered questioningly as if that had not occurred to him.

John Daniel, rugged and grim, wanted to pray but felt that this was not a time to suggest it. So far as he was concerned it was the only solution.

Bill replied uncertainly. 'Over the fall. I'm going to climb it. Give me that lamp.'

'You'll never reach the top,' Iestyn argued, shaking his head.

Shoni mumbled agreement, while Tommy's fingers were curled in Dick's leather belt as he stood behind him.

'Better wait a bit,' Dick cautioned.

John Daniel felt the time had come to ask for Divine help. 'God will help us out,' he said dispassionately. 'Same as He got us in.'

'Give me that lamp!' Bill screamed, his face distorted with passion. He pushed Iestyn in the chest, making him trip over a sleeper, releasing the lamp.

'Hold him!' Iestyn cried, his voice tense with pain. His buttocks hurt.

Bill ran towards the fall, ducking to avoid the boulder under which Dick had peeped. His head went past, but his shoulder struck it, bringing down a mass of earth and stones on top of him. His legs slowly straightened themselves, scales of rock sliding down under the pressure of his toes. His lamp lit stones and posts with a mysterious white glare.

Hurriedly Iestyn and Dick and John Daniel scraped away the rubbish. Bill's scalp hung loose. Iestyn felt his heart, saying after a while, 'Can't feel anything much. I think he's dead.'

Dick asked, 'Can't we do nothing for him?' He thought that there should be something.

'What can we do?'

They laid Bill at the side of the road, between the tram-lines and the timber. Iestyn took off his own sweat-soaked shirt and put it over Bill's bloodstreaked head. He laid it there reverently and gently, as if afraid the body might feel roughness from his touch. They all thought something should be done, yet did not know what. The time had not come for a hymn or a committal. Bill was still with them – he hadn't been from them. It was just as if he had fallen asleep.

Wearily Iestyn settled himself on the ground again. The others did likewise.

It was getting hotter and hotter, and breathing was difficult. All were weak and wet with sweat. They sat or lay around, muttering and moaning, and taking frequent sips of the water left in their tin jacks. Iestyn shared that of the others. Dick had one arm across Tommy who lay on his stomach with his cheek upon the man's grimy trousers. Bill's death had meant nothing to him when it had occurred, being natural to life underground. But now something was stirring within him, disturbing and depressing. Shoni rose and staggered into the gloom. The others could hear him vomiting.

After a while Dick muttered, 'Hell's bells. I'll be spewing with him if he don't stop.'

Iestyn, too, was afraid to open his mouth in case he also became sick. John Daniel was silent.

Shoni came back, wiping the clinging saliva from his lips.

His throat burned and there were tears in his eyes.

'Ugh, no good,' he said, shaking his head. 'Can't get it up although I want to. Shoved my fingers down and all.'

Tommy turned his head from the damp familiarity of Dick's trousers. 'When they going to get us out, Dick?' he asked. 'How they going to do it?'

'I don't know, bach,' Dick replied, giving the boy's shoulder an assuring squeeze. 'But they'll find somehow to do it. I expect they're working on it now outside of the fall.'

John Daniel rose ponderously to his feet. Not tall, he was broad and heavy.

'There's one way we haven't tried,' he proclaimed. 'We haven't prayed. Let us pray to God for guidance and hope – that he brings us safely out of this great danger.'

Iestyn turned on his side, feeling too ill to be interested. The others watched apathetically.

John Daniel got down on his knees and began praying aloud, a mystic figure in the gloom. With a confident voice he began, 'Father in Heaven, we ask Thee to be our Guide and Strength as Thou wast the Guide and Strength of the Israelities in the wilderness, and of Daniel in the flaming fire . . .'

The sight of his worshipping body and the sound of his resonant voice filled Tommy with uncontrollable fear. He sobbed violently on Dick's breast, his arms around his neck.

Dick sat up. 'Stop it, John Daniels,' he cried. 'Stop it, will you. You'll drive this kid balmy if you don't stop, and me with him.'

But John Daniel went on, his voice rich with urgent supplication. 'We are in Thy hands, O Lord, and need Thy comfort which even Thy Beloved Son did not have upon the Cross. But we ask it now, O Lord – '

'Stop it, I tell you!' Dick cried again, rising to one knee, Tommy still clinging around his neck. 'I don't want no bloody God hanging around me. If He wanted to get us out of here He wouldn't have got us into it. If He ent man enough to get us out of a mess like this of His own accord when this kid's here He can keep his bloody miracles.'

John Daniel stopped aghast. 'Don't you blaspheme, Richard Jones,' he rebuked. 'We should thank God in an hour like this that our lives have been spared and that we got strength left to try and get out.'

'We're not out yet by a hell of a long way, butty, and don't you forget it. And I suppose we got to thank God for getting us out of what He got us into. If I get out I'll thank the bloke that gets me out, not somebody that's floating around in the air making trouble and then having to be asked to give a hand to shift it.'

'Richard Jones' – there was cold dignity in the voice – 'you are a wicked man. A very wicked man. And some day will come a judgment that will make you realise your folly – when it is too late.'

Throwing Tommy aside Dick rose to his feet, his face furrowed with rage.

'I hope you're right,' he shouted. 'And when I'm up for judgment I'll have a bit of straight talk to give Him, too, even if I have to rot in hell for it. Making kids like Tommy here to come down and work in a bastard hole like this – and for life, too – is bad enough, but to get him in a jam like this as well . . . You . . .' He drew his fist back to strike the man who stood resolutely in front of him.

Iestyn and Shoni were on their feet. Shoni slipped his arm around Dick's neck from behind, while Iestyn got between the quarrelling men.

'Haven't you two got anything better to do at a time like this?' Iestyn asked bitterly. 'Sit down, you pair of bloody fools. Sit down, John, and if you want to pray, pray to yourself. God will hear you that way as well as any other. You, of all people, ought to have more sense.'

John Daniel turned away. The others lay down, even more exhausted than before. Tommy crept back to Dick. 'Don't quarrel again. Dick,' he begged. 'You won't, will you?'

Tears flowed down Dick's cheeks. He felt weak; his emotions were near the surface, 'All right, Tommy bach,' he muttered.

'We won't quarrel again, will we, John?'

John Daniel looked across at them, his puritanical face like carved stone.

'No, we won't quarrel again, Richard Jones,' he replied. 'Quarrelling is a very wicked thing.'

Iestyn came to himself with a start. His head hung back and his mouth was open and dry. He had been asleep, but did not know for how long. He felt ill and dazed.

A faint, familiar smell made him raise his tired head and sniff. His tongue touched his cracked lips.

'Gas!' he tried to say aloud, but managed only to shape the words.

With a weary hand he lifted the iron lamp which seemed almost too heavy to lift, and peered around. There was no sound; the others must be sleeping. He listened for the jingle of Duke's harness, for he could not see him, but there was nothing but intense, echoing silence.

'Gas,' his lips said again; 'the place is full of it.'

He clambered laboriously to his feet, climbing up his legs with his hands. His body ached. He wanted water but could not remember where the jacks were. Perhaps they were on the other side of the road; he tried to get there. His head reeled and he was able to move only a few inches at a time. He almost collapsed, and had to cling to the side for support.

'Pull – your – self – to – geth – er,' he mumbled almost inaudibly. He rested his back against the timber and tried to clear his mind. He knew the others were being asphyxiated, and wondered if he should warn them. But even his fuddled brain realised that waking them to a knowledge of their danger would not help them.

Again he tried to get the water, but had barely taken his weight off the post when his knees began to sag. He fought against it, struggling to keep himself from sliding to the ground.

'Mustn't . . . sit . . . down,' he mouthed, wiping his lips with his wrist and forearm. 'Mustn't . . . sit down . . . or . . .

I'll go to sleep and . . . and never wake up.'

Lights raced upward before his eyes in glittering streaks. He crumpled and fell on his side, his knees twisted and bent, his head lolling back.

He sighed. A trickle of saliva rolled slowly across his cheek from the corner of his mouth.

The racing lights merged into one motionless yellow flame, like a huge altar candle . . .

The fall of earth stretched up to where the seam above had been worked away.

Coal seams were like shelves in a cupboard, but with earth between them instead of air. Some were worked more quickly than others, as this upper one had been.

It did not take long for the shaking of the intervening ground by passing horses and trams to loosen the thin crust of earth, forming a hole which increased continuously, letting the gas escape from the lower seam. In time comparatively fresh air took its place, and the gas had disappeared almost entirely before the hole was discovered by men working in the upper seam.

When the fireman in charge there arrived with a hastily assembled working party he tested the ground with his foot, one man holding his hand and a third forming another link in the human chain in case he fell through.

In the hole itself, tramrails sagged from lack of support and one sleeper hung down with only a bent nail holding it. As the fireman stamped his foot the rail fell away and skidded raggedly down the fall.

After several unsuccessful attempts the ground remained firm enough for him to wriggle through the hole and down on the massive, rugged heap. In his hand he carried an oil-lamp for testing gas, while a heavy electric one hung from his belt.

Down the fall he went, stones and earth sliding away under his weight. He soon had to shift the oil lamp to his mouth, the curved handle gripped between his teeth. Then he travelled on hands and toes and stomach. The stones cut his hands.

At the bottom he paused to regain his breath.

'You O.K. there, Dai?' a voice called from above.

'Aye, but don't come down yet; I'll tell you when to come.'

'O.K.'

After some moments he went carefully and laboriously from man to man as they lay around. Iestyn was between the tram-lines. Tommy was embracing Dick; his cap had fallen off, and his face showed calm and serene through a film of coaldust. Shoni, in his football jersey, had his mouth open as if in an eternal snore. John Daniel was on his knees in an attitude of prayer. Duke was a massive heap on the ground. Dai listened to their hearts, even that of the horse.

When he got to Bill he removed Iestyn's shirt. 'Duw, Duw,' he murmured with awe. 'He must have had a hell of a clout.'

Then he listened to Bill's heart. Bill was the last. He listened for a long time . . .

The manager arrived at the edge of the hole above. 'What's it like down there, Dai?' he called, preparing to follow. 'Are they all right?'

'No,' came the echoing reply; 'they're . . . all dead.'

'What! All of them?'

'Aye, all of them – except one. Bill Rees the fireman's still alive. There was a wet shirt over his face, and it kept the gas out and saved him. And he's mumbling something about some Black Goddess who's laughing at something . . .'

THE DEVIL'S TREE
EGLWYS RHOS, NEAR LLANDUDNO

At the corner of the first turning after passing the village of Llanrhos, on the left hand side, is a withered oak tree, called by the natives of those parts the Devil's Tree, and it was thought to be haunted, and therefore the young and timid were afraid to pass it of a dark night.

Its bad reputation was greatly increased by an occurrence

that happened there to Cadwaladr Williams, a shoemaker, who lived at Llansantffraid Glan Conway.

This shoemaker sometimes refreshed himself too freely before starting homewards from Llandudno, and he was in the habit of turning into the public house at Llanrhos to gain courage to pass the Devil's Tree.

One Saturday night instead of quietly passing this tree on the other side, he walked fearlessly up to it, and defied the Evil One to appear if he was there. No sooner had he uttered the defiant words than something fell from the tree, and lit upon his shoulders, and grasped poor Cadwaladr's neck with a grip of iron. He fought with the incubus savagely to get rid of it, but all his exertions were in vain, and so he was obliged to proceed on his journey with this fearful thing clinging to him, which became heavier and heavier every step he took. At last, thoroughly exhausted, he came to Towyn, and, more dead than alive, he reached a friend's door and knocked, and oh, what pleasure, before the door was opened the weight on his back had gone, but his friend knew who it was that Cadwaladr had carried from the Devil's Tree.

From *Welsh Folk-lore* by Rev. Elias Owen, M.A., F.S.A., 1887

THE STRANGER

RICHARD HUGHES

The street in Cylfant was so steep that if you took a middling jump from the top of the village you would not touch ground again till you reached the bottom : but you would probably hurt yourself. The houses sat each on other's left shoulder, all the way up, so that the smoke from Mrs Grocery-Jones's chimney blew in at Mrs Boot-Jones's basement, and out through her top windows into the cellar of the Post Office, and out through the Post Office Daughter's little bedroom casement into that of the Butchery Aunt (who was paralysed and lived downstairs): and so on, up the whole line like a flue, till it left soot on the stomachs of the sheep grazing on the hillside above.

But that does not explain why the stranger came to Cylfant village, unless it was through curiosity: nor, indeed, what he was doing in such a Sabbath-keeping little Anabaptist hamlet at all, where he might have known he would meet with an accident: nor what he was doing so far from home.

Mr Williams was the rector of Cylfant, and perhaps thirty miles round: such an old fat man that he had difficulty in walking between his different churches on Sundays. His face was heavy, his eyes small but with a dream in them, and he kept sticky sweet things ready in his pocket. He was stone deaf, so that now he roared like a bull, now whispered like a young lover. He might be heard roaring across a valley. He had one black suit, with patches on it, and one surplice, that he darned sometimes. He lived by letting the rectory in the summer: and when the Disestablishment Bill wiped away his stipend of eight pounds, he made up for it by taking in washing: you would see him in front of the rectory, legs set well apart, both heavy arms plunged up to the elbows in suds, a towel pinned to each shoulder to save his black coat, roaring a greeting to all who might pass.

Cylfant was very proud of the smallness of his congregation: for in Wales to have many church-people in a village is a great disgrace. They are always the scallywags, the folk who have been expelled from their chapels; and who hope, even if they cannot expect heaven, that things will not be quite so uncomfortable for them in the next world as if they gave up religion altogether. There were only three families, except for the Squire's governess, that ever came to Cylfant church. Mr Williams hated verse, but he preached them pure poetry: he had such an imagination that if he meditated on the anatomy of angels there seemed to be strange flying things about his head; and the passionate roaring and whispering of his voice could hang Christ even on the polished brass altar-cross.

Presently he married the girl who played the harmonium:

but she had one leg.

It was she, Minnie, that took in the Stranger. They were sitting one night in the rectory parlour, and Mr Williams was reading a book of sermons with great fixity of mind, in order to forget his Loss: for that day the little ring on his watch-chain had opened, and he had lost the gold cross that he had always carried. Minnie was sure that it had been there when they started to climb the village: but they had no lantern: the wind was a fleet howling darkness, so they could not search till the morning, even if it lay on their very doorstep. Mr Williams read three sermons at a gulp, and closed the book. It was always a thing of amazement that a man who read such dull sermons with such avidity could put so much thrill and beauty, so little of the moralities, into his own preaching.

He shut the book, and, giving a great sigh, puffed out his cheeks, while he squinted along the broad shirt-front under his chin. Minnie went to turn down the lamp – as she always did, for reasons of thrift, when her husband was not actually reading; and all at once she heard a cry in the night, sharp as a child's, and full of terror and innocence. She opened the door, and saw a small huddled figure in the roadway. There was a little light shining from it, bluish and fitful: and she knew at once it was something more than natural. She set her wooden leg firmly against the doorstep, and, bending down, caught the Stranger up in her arms, and lifted him over the threshold. He lay there, blinking in the lamplight: a grotesque thing, with misshapen ears and a broad, flat nose. His limbs were knotted, but the skin at his joints was yellow and delicate as a snake's belly. He had crumpled wings, as fine as petrol upon water: even thus battered, their beauty could not but be seen. He seemed in pain: and there was a small cross-shaped weal burnt on his side, as if he had stumbled on a little red-hot iron.

'Poor little thing,' said Mr Williams, looking at it sideways from his chair. 'What is it?'

'It is more ugly than anything I have ever seen,' said Minnie. 'Perhaps it is an angel: for it was never born of woman.'

'We should be more humble, Minnie,' said her husband.

'Who are we that God should send His angels to try us?'

'At any rate, I think it is not,' said Minnie. 'We will see.'

She took up the book of sermons, and touched him on the forehead with it. He gave a shrill yell of pain.

'God forgive me for my cruelty,' she exclaimed. 'It must be a – '

'It is a Stranger,' said Mr Williams quickly.

Minnie turned and looked at him.

'What shall we do?' she shouted in his ear. 'For if we harbour it we shall surely be damned. We must not help God's enemies.'

'We are taught to love our enemies,' whispered Mr Williams. 'And who is God's enemy is ours too.'

'But it can feel no gratitude,' said Minnie. 'It will return us evil for good.'

'If we do good in the hope of gratitude we have our reward,' roared Mr Williams.

'You mean you will keep him?' said Minnie.

'I mean' – the old man groaned – 'I do not know what to do, indeed, whatever.'

But the visitor settled that question for them himself. He crawled over to the fireplace, and sitting himself on one of the reddest coals, smiled out at them with a grin that stretched from ear to ear.

II

That was how the little devil came to Cylfant rectory. He had great natural charm, and when the cross-shaped weal on his side was better – for it healed quickly under the action of fire – his spirits returned to him. One was led to forget the grotesque beauty of his form by the generous amiability of his expression. He took to the old rector at once; and Mr Williams himself could not but feel a secret liking for him. That night he followed them up to bed: Mr Williams had to shut and lock the bedroom door on him. But hardly were they inside when they saw a bluish light on the panel: and presently the little devil was sitting perched upon the bed-rail, watching with a sober interest Minnie unstrap her wooden leg: and even when she said her prayers – which she did in a shamefast fashion, for fear of giving him pain – he showed no embarrassment whatever. When they were both fast asleep, he took down Minnie's old peg from the shelf where she had laid it, and did something to it in the corner. He then lay down in a pool of moonlight, and was still sleeping soundly when the rector heaved himself out of bed in the morning. The old man woke Minnie, who scrambled out of bed, and began to strap on her leg preparatory to getting the breakfast; but a wonderful thing happened, for no sooner had she fitted her scarred stump into the leather socket than the leather changed to flesh, and the wood to flesh, and there she was with the most elegant and seductive leg that ever troubled a man's eye: and, moreover, there was a silk stocking on it, and a high-heeled Paris shoe on it, before she could recover from her surprise. As she drew on her old ringed black-and-white cotton oddment over the other stocky red ankle she thought that never had such a pair of legs been seen together on one body. She looked round in a guilty fashion: but her husband was balanced in front of the looking-glass shaving himself. He had not seen. She pulled on her dress all in a hurry and danced away downstairs. She let up the blinds and swept the floor; and all the time her new leg behaved as well as if she had known it all her life: but directly she flung open the front door to shake the mat, it began all at once to drag, and jib: she got pins and needles in it: it jumped and kicked like a thing quite out of control. And she saw the reason: for there in the roadway, where she had found the Stranger the night before, was the rector's gold cross.

'There is no mistaking,' said Minnie to herself, 'where *that* leg came from.'

And, indeed, there was not. She sidled up to the cross with difficulty, and recovered it: and all at once heard steps on the cobbles. It was Scraggy Evan, the postman. Minnie's first thought was to hide the leg, for it would take some explaining away. But it would not be hidden: the shameless thing thrust the delicate turn of its ankle right under Scraggy Evan's nose. Scraggy's cheery 'bore da!' was lost in a gasp, and poor Minnie fled into the house scarlet with shame, the damnable leg giving coquettish little kicks into the air as she went.

What Scraggy told the village we can only guess: but he must have told them something, or why should Mrs Williams have received so many callers that morning? The first came when breakfast was hardly over: and the Stranger was sitting quietly on the hob picking his teeth with his tail. Minnie had great presence of mind. She ran to her work-box, and taking from it a red-flannel petticoat that she had been mending, wrapped the Stranger in it and crammed him quickly into a wooden box, begging him in a staccato whisper to lie still. Upon the face of Mr Williams there was a look of much courage and resignation. Devil or no, he was prepared to justify his guest to all comers. Minnie opened the door, and Mrs Grocery-Jones stood there.

'Good morning,' said she. 'I was calling to ask if you are driving over to Ynysllanbedrbachdeudraethgerylan today.'

She paused and sniffed; then sniffed again.

There was no doubt of it: somewhere sulphur was burning.

'We are not,' said Minnie. 'We are too busy here, indeed, with the plaguy wasps. Mr Williams has hardly smoked out one nest, but bad are they as they were before, indeed.'

Mrs Jones gave a gasp of surprise.

'Wasps in the winter-time?' she said.

'I did not say *wasps*,' said Minnie, 'I said the *wallpaper*, which the doctor thinks may have the scarlet fever lurking in it, so have we fumigated the whole house.'

It was lucky, thought Minnie, that her husband was so deaf. He would never have forgiven her.

'Well, good gracious!' said Mrs Jones. As her eyes got used to the dim light she caught sight of a broad head with two beady yellow eyes, peering at her from a soap-box. 'And is that a cat you have there, Mrs Williams?'

'It is a *pig*!' she cried with sudden heat; for her new leg showed an obvious desire to kick Mrs Jones out of the house.

'It has the wind,' she explained, 'so we thought it would be best in the house, indeed.'

'Well, good gracious me!' repeated Mrs Jones.

Minnie's leg was quivering, but she managed to control it. Mrs Jones was staring past her at the pig as if she could not take her eyes off it. As, indeed, she could not: for suddenly she shot half across the road, backwards, with the force of a bullet: and when released she scrambled down the street, as she herself explained it, 'as if the devil was after me': and there was the Stranger, wrapped still in the red-flannel petticoat sitting on the window-sill and grinning amiably at her back.

III

If Mr Williams had lived longer, a few curious things might have happened in Cylfant village: but he did not. There was a buzzing feeling in his head all that day, and when he went to bed at night he lay quietly on his back staring at the ceiling. It had turned a bright green. Presently, with his eyes open still, he began to snore. Minnie did not notice anything queer; and in the small hours of the morning, after two or three loud snorts, he stopped altogether.

When he felt better, he found that his soul was outside his body. It was not at all the kind of thing he had expected it to be, but was fairly round, and made of some stuff like white of egg. He gathered it gently into his arms, and began to float about: his body had disappeared. Presently he was aware that the Stranger was still watching him.

'You'll be damned for this: double-damned even, for giving place to the devil – and you a priest.' He sighed. 'It is so hard,' he went on seriously, 'even for devils to conquer their better nature. Oh, I *try* hard enough. I surely try. The seeds of goodness have lurked in us ever since the Fall; try as we will, they *sprout*.

'"*With a fork drive Nature out,*
She will ever yet return."

'Temptation is always lurking ready for us: it is a long and a hard fight: the Forces of Evil against the Forces of Good. But we shall conquer in the end: with Wrong on our side, we *must* conquer.' There was an elation in his face that transcended all earthly ugliness. 'At last,' he went on, 'I have done a really immoral act: an act with no trace of good in it, either in motive or effect. You will be damned, and Minnie will be damned too, even if she has to hop to hell on the leg I gave her. But it was hard, hard.'

Old Williams floated over on to the other side.

'I am a sinful man,' he said; 'a very sinful man. Heaven was never my deserts, whatever.'

The devil looked at him in surprise.

'Oh, you were not!' he said earnestly. 'Indeed, you were not! You were the truest – '

He stopped suddenly. Williams was aware of the presence of some very unpleasant personality. He looked round: and behind him stood a tall figure with thin, tight lips and watery eyes, who began speaking at once – rapidly, as if by rote.

'As a matter of form,' said he, 'I claim this soul.'

'As a matter of form,' replied the devil in a sing-song voice, 'he is mine.'

The angel rapped out: 'De qua causa?'

'De diabolo consortando,' chaunted the little devil, in even worse Latin.

'Quae sit evidentia?'

'Tuos voco oculos ipsos.'

'Quod vidi, vero, atque affirmo – Satis,' continued the angel 'Tuumst.' And he turned to go.

'Stop!' cried the Stranger suddenly, all his bad resolutions breaking down.

'Stop!' he cried, and began speaking rapidly. 'I'm a backslider, I know, but the strain is too much: there's no true devilry in me. Take him: take him: there never was better Christian in Wales, I swear it: and to that alone his damnation is due: pure charity – '

'What are you talking about?' snapped the angel petulantly.

'The case is settled: I have withdrawn my claim.'

'So do I!' cried the devil excitedly. 'I withdraw mine.'

The angel shrugged his wings.

'What's the use of making a scene?' he said. 'Never, in all my office, have I known a fiend break down and forget himself like this before. You are making an exhibition of yourself, sir! Besides, if we both withdraw, he can't go anywhere. It's none of my business.'

He shrugged his wings and soared away.

'*Heaven or Hell or the Land of Whipperginny*,' murmured Williams to himself, vague memories of Nashe rising to the surface of his astonishment. Together they watched the angel's purple pinions bearing him from sight: the Stranger cocked a snook at his straight back.

'Where now?' asked the rector.

'Where now? Heaven! Wait till he's out of sight.'

He turned and winked broadly at Williams, making a motion on his bare shanks as if to thrust his hand in a pocket.

'You come with me,' he said. 'I know how I can get things fixed for you!'

A PERILOUS STRUGGLE

One skilled man thus related his perilous experience in laying a ghost on one occasion when he had mistaken the grade of the troubler. 'You have heard speak of the ghost of Erw,' said he; 'it was an awful ghost, one of the worst that I have ever heard of. He became so exceedingly troublesome that the family had to give up the house, which was closed for some years in the hope that the ghost would go away. But on seeing that this did not avail, and that instead of becoming better the ghost became much worse, the man came to me to ask my advice. I promised to go and put him down.

'One evening – I shall never forget it – I went thither, and entered the house; I then made the mystical circle on the floor with salt, and drew the image of the cross in its centre. Then I entered the circle myself and stood between the arms of the cross in the customary way, reading the usual charm passage. Almost instantly the door is flung back, and some hideous creature, not unlike a huge tiger, enters, gnashing its terrible teeth at me. It then turned around the circle, as much as to say, 'I have got thee now'. I immediately perceived that I had mistaken its grade, and that I had used too low a summons. But I stood like steel before him, showing not the slightest bit of fear, and ordered him to withdraw in the name of the cross on which I stood, or else that I would curse him with endless torture. He stood unmoved, and there we remained for a long time staring at one another, until at last I could see him gradually withdrawing. I then instantly changed one word in the charm passage, and he came back, licking the floor like a dog before his master. I pronounced his sentence and sacrificed him to the bottom of Llyn Du; and while there is water in that lake he will never come forth to trouble any one again. That was the last spirit with which I had to do, or will have to do. If I had betrayed the least bit of fear, or if I had taken my eye off for the quarter of a second, I would have been done for.'

From *Bedd Gelert, its Facts, Fairies, and Folk-lore,*
by D. E. Jenkins, 1899

LORD DUNWILLIAM AND THE CWN ANNWN

R. CHETWYND-HAYES

My Lord Dunwilliam was not, to say the least, in a good mood. The interior of the coach was cold, the road, if the snow-covered track could be so designated, was rough, and his lordship was tossed upwards, then flung from side to side, and the coachman, who was steadily freezing high up on his elevated seat, trembled as Dunwilliam gave vent to his rage.

'Blind, blockheaded cretin, drive round the bloody holes, not in them.'

Had he been given the gift of free speech, Coggins, for such was the coachman's name, might well have pointed out that in a blinding snowstorm it was a miracle that he had so far kept the coach on four wheels, but not being so gifted he did his best to guide the team of four horses on what he devoutly trusted was the centre of the road. His trust was misplaced.

The coach reeled over, then slid into what appeared to be a deep ditch; the horses screamed as they were pulled backwards, and Coggins fell from his perch and landed in a deep pile of snow. He clambered to his feet and hastened to aid his employer, whose scarlet face was glaring at him from the remains of the near-side window.

'You blasted, addle-brained imbecile.' His lordship was impelled to desist while he made the perilous descent from tilted coach to snow-coated road, then he took a deep breath and continued. 'You walled-eye son of Jezebel, you maggot-ridden ball of excreta, what by the devil and all his angels do you think you're doing?'

'Snow, me Lord.' Coggins spoke quickly, knowing he had little time before the next outburst. 'Ditch, me Lord, couldn't see it, me Lord.'

'A ditch,' Lord Dunwilliam pointed out with assumed patience, 'is for draining water into. A road is intended for driving coaches on. Those little bags of moisture situated on either side of your misshapened nose are called eyes. They are supposed to inform that minute spec of putrescence that you in all seriousness call a brain, which is which.'

The enormity of his crime came home to Coggins, and he could only mutter: 'Beg pardon, me Lord. Beg pardon.'

'Where are we?' Dunwilliam pulled his greatcoat tighter about his burly form.

'So far as I can ascertain,' Coggins was releasing the struggling horses, 'half-way between Llanwddyn and Bala.'

'Right, saddle Lucifer. I'll sleep in Bala tonight or die in the attempt.'

'But, me Lord,' Coggins wiped the snow from his eyes, 'it's all of eight miles, and you have to cross the Berwyn Mountains, and there'll be deep drifts by now.'

'Get the saddle out of the boot.' Dunwilliam spat snow out of his mouth. 'Then my valise.'

'My Lord,' Coggins protested again, 'in a few hours it'll be as black as the devil's hand. I know this country and, begging your pardon, your lordship does not, and I would not make such a journey alone on a night like this. If you must go on, turn east and make for Llangynog.'

'Saddle the horse and don't talk so much,' Dunwilliam instructed. 'I meet my man of business in Bala tomorrow, and that will not be possible if I go to Llangynog tonight.'

Ten minutes later found Lord Dunwilliam seated upon the leading coachhorse, gazing down at his coachman with an impatient frown.

'What shall I do, my Lord?' Coggins said.

'Do, man, do? First get blankets from the boot for the horses, then see they are hobbled in a sheltered spot. Afterwards, I suppose you'd better take cover in the coach, always supposing you can sit or lie at an angle. I'll send someone back when I get to Bala.'

Lord Dunwilliam rode away without a single backward glance, and it seemed the snow was eager to erase the footprints of his horse.

It caressed his eyes with icy fingers, it cloyed his nostrils, clogged his ears, clung to his horse's hoofs and mocked his impotent rage. The wind swept down from the Berwyn Mountains, driving the snow before it like a plague of white moths, and it screamed a terrible cry that was at times one of desolate despair, at others one of unholy joy. Dunwilliam on several occasions was almost lifted out of his saddle, and it was then that he clung to the horse's neck, digging his toes well under it's belly, swearing aloud, for his lordship was a man who always coated his fear with a thick layer of anger. He had been riding, if that was the correct expression for this slow plodding, for an hour – maybe two; the light was failing, and he was, without any possible doubt, hopelessly lost. But even now he had no regrets, he did not blame himself for setting out on this nightmare journey. He had to be in Bala before morning, and he blamed the wind, the snow, the night that was falling too soon, for his predicament. Even when he knew death was shrieking in on the wind, striking at his exhausted body with grave-cold fingers, there was no relenting from his purpose, no thought of stopping, surrendering to the nigh-overwhelming need to bed down in a soft blanket of snow and sleep for ever.

Perhaps it was the horse that instinctively made for the only house within ten miles, or maybe Dunwilliam's own sense of self-preservation was sufficiently developed for him to steer his horse in the right direction, or maybe he was just lucky, but suddenly he found himself peering at a lighted window that was only a few yards in front. A window, a rectangle of light, and next to it was a green door, now daintily framed with crisp snow, and somehow Dunwilliam was pounding upon it, roaring out his demand: 'By the devil and all his angels let me in,' and his cry was eagerly seized by the wind and hurled back to the glowering mountains.

The door opened and he fell forward into a world of warmth and light; the voices had that soft Welsh lilt he had sometimes found rather irritating, but now they were telling him he had stumbled past the gates of death, that his flesh would not freeze, his heart continue to pump, his senses could still function.

He was in a chair by a roaring log fire, an oil-lamp with a frosted globe casting a soft radiance round the small room, keeping shadows at bay, and making golden-edged patterns on the ceiling.

'I've put your horse in the barn, so don't fret yourself.'

It was a short, stocky man who spoke; a bald-headed fellow, with a strong, pugnacious face, attired in a coarse shirt of unbleached linen, and well-worn corduroy trousers. He blinked down at his unexpected guest and Dunwilliam detected a hint of hostility in the small blue eyes.

'Good of you.' He struggled to sit upright, and was alarmed to find he was weak, trembling like a sere leaf in an autumn wind. 'Lost out there, lucky I stumbled across your cottage.'

'Indeed, you must have been mad, man, to be abroad on a night like this. No more sense than you were born with, I'm thinking, and it's a wonder you aren't stark and cold in a blanket of snow – if not worse.'

'What!' A frown creased Dunwilliam's brow; no one had spoken to him in such a fashion for twenty years. 'I go where I please, when I please, and damn the insolence of any man who questions that fact. I am Lord Dunwilliam.'

'And I am Evan ap Evans, a prince in my own house, and I'll damn any man, be he king or commoner, who raises his voice to me . . .'

'Dadda, hush yourself,' a soft voice interrupted, 'he is tired and speaks without meaning offence. Calm yourself and see to the old fire.'

Evans grunted, then turned in the direction of the fire as Dunwilliam twisted his head to see who had so aptly poured oil on stormy waters, then froze into an attitude of profound astonishment.

She was perhaps eighteen, with the slim grace of a gazelle. A mist of raven hair framed her pale face, and her eyes were dark, without expression, as they gave the burly, but handsome man one swift glance. Her beauty was so vivid and, in some inexplicable way, unearthly, that Dunwilliam experienced a spasm of pain. He was a product of his age and caste; he seduced women of his own class with a certain brutal charm. Those below the salt he just took. But here he knew was an exception; the girl walked and spoke with a gentle naïve dignity, and would not be impressed by either his rank or purse: indeed, it soon became apparent she had little interest in him at all.

'I will get you something to eat.' The voice was low, soft, the Welsh lilt barely perceptible. 'Then I'll make you up some sort of bed before the fire for, to be sure, you'll not be going out again tonight.'

'I'm obliged to you, Mam.' Dunwilliam nodded, his eyes ravaging the pale face, vainly trying to find some flaw, some imperfection, so as to subdue the pain, but the skin was smooth and clear; the high cheekbones would not have disgraced Aphrodite herself. 'I'm on my way to Bala, must meet my man of business there tomorrow. I've just inherited an estate thereabouts.'

'Indeed.'

She put a large saucepan on the trivet, then went to a dresser and took down plates before proceeding to lay the table.

'Dadda, can you not make yourself useful? We'll need some more logs if the poor man is not to freeze.'

Evan ap Evans growled, then obediently trudged heavily from the room.

'It must be lonely for you out here.' Dunwilliam was trying to make conversation, say anything to attract the girl's attention, and he experienced an unreasoning spasm of anger when she did not even turn her head but continued to lay the table.

'No, I have much to do. Only the idle are lonely.'

'Damnation, girl!' his voice rose, then with an effort he regained self control. 'Surely you crave some kind of social life? People your own age, a bit of gaiety? What the hell do you do with yourself in this God-forsaken place?'

'I walk.' She moved over to the fireplace so that her slim, but mature, form was silhouetted against the fluttering flames. 'I listen to the voices in the wind.'

'Have you no lover – no sweetheart?'

'That, sir, is my affair.'

The rebuke was made in the same cool voice, as though she were snubbing an insolent schoolboy whose ill-manners were the result of ignorance rather than ill-intent, and his anger grew.

'I but asked a civil question.'

'And I replied with a civil answer.' She walked, or rather

glided, to the door. 'Dadda, the food is ready to be served, and you'll catch your death out there.'

Evan ap Evans appeared, a pile of logs supported by his outstretched arms; his face was like a thunder cloud as he let them fall to the hearth.

'Must you call me as though I were a dog being summoned to its meat? I'm not a servant to come and go as you bid, but your father to respect and obey, and I'm telling you not to forget it.'

She put her arms around this ugly bear of a man, and gently laid her lips on his weather beaten cheek, and Dunwilliam saw the bleak little eyes soften.

'She rules him with a rod of velvet,' he told himself. 'He'll rant and roar, then try to kill the man who looks at her.'

'Be seated at table.' The words were a command, and Dunwilliam rose to his feet, then seated himself at the rough deal table, determined that he would not look at her, but his eyes seemed unable to remove their burning gaze from that pale, calm face.

The meal was a stew – meat, vegetables, mainly potatoes – all boiled together in one pot, followed by a portion of strong cheese and hard biscuits, but Dunwilliam ate well, for his journey through the snow had made him ravenous, and he was in no mood to be fastidious. Evan ap Evans was not a silent eater; he smacked his lips, belched, made obscene gurgling sounds, while the girl chewed daintily with closed lips and never once raised her eyes in Dunwilliam's direction.

'You live alone with your daughter?' He addressed Evans, who did not seem over-pleased at being disturbed while at meat. 'Your good wife, am I to understand . . .?'

'Partaker of glory,' Evans roared with full mouth.

'What!'

'She's been a partaker of glory these past ten years. The cold got her, and she crossed the broad river on a night such as this.'

'My condolences.' Dunwilliam watched the girl and thought of snow on a mountain peak; her face was composed, devoid of expression, a white canvas, and he suddenly wanted to make her angry, hurt her, do anything that would crumble that beautiful mask. He spoke loudly, glaring at her while Evans scraped his plate clean with a spoon.

'But no doubt your daughter has taken her place, and sees to your comforts as is her duty.'

Neither father nor daughter answered him, and Dunwilliam, spurred on by his great pain, allowed the words to come tumbling from his tongue.

'But the time will come when some young fellow will pick your Welsh flower and carry it away to decorate his bed and board, and then you will have only the cold comfort of memories.'

Evan ap Evans raised his head very slowly and stared at his guest with eyes like chips of blue ice; Dunwilliam tensed his muscles, but Evans merely said out of the corner of his mouth:

'Silah, fetch the ale.'

The girl rose, collected the plates together in one pile, then carried them into the kitchen.

'So, that is her name,' Dunwilliam said. 'Silah. It suits her.'

'I am thinking,' remarked Evans in a low voice, 'you have been bitten by sharp teeth. The poison is in your blood and soon you will howl like a mad dog.'

'You forget yourself, fellow.' Dunwilliam clenched his fists, and there was an expression on his face that would have made Coggins tremble. 'I am Lord Dunwilliam, a close friend of the Prince Regent, and I do not howl for a peasant girl.'

Evan ap Evans bared his teeth.

'Look you, man, I care not if you are mad George himself, lay but a hand on her and you'll live to curse the day your mother cleansed her womb of your presence.'

'You dare to threaten me?' Lord Dunwilliam half rose from his chair, his face scarlet with anger, and Evans chuckled.

'There's no need to roar and vomit your rage upon me. But there is another, more stronger than I . . .' He began to nod, jerked his head up and down as though emphasising some bitter undeniable truth. 'Indeed yes, another much stronger, who would have you shrieking out your guts within the hour.'

'Who is this bully boy?' Dunwilliam demanded. 'A lover?'

Evans stared at the snow-curtained window; there was naked fear in his eyes now, and his voice was harsh, barely above a whisper.

'You may say so. A lover.'

'Know you,' Dunwilliam leant forward, and now he looked dangerous, powerful, his great hands balled up into fists, 'I am well able to give a good account of myself. 'Tis not a soft band who wait upon his Highness back there in Whitehall. The noble art is much practised, and I laid Jem Turner, champion of all England, upon his back in the eighth round, and won ten thousand guineas into the bargain. Fists, cudgels, swords, I'll take on any two men at once and come off best, so don't try to frighten me with her bully lover.'

Evans laughed, a loud, mirthless roar, and pulled up the sleeve of his shirt, baring his forearm.

'Look you.' He pointed to three livid scars that ran the entire length of his arm from wrist to elbow. 'I but took the stick to her, for does not the good book say "the father who loves his child must chastise"? Had she not pleaded for me, I would now be adding my voice to the cry of despair that is borne in on the night storm. But you . . . Should you do that which lurks in your mind, I would pity you. Aye, I'm a hard man, with little softness, but for you I would weep tears of compassion.'

'There is madness in your brain,' Dunwilliam whispered. 'Living alone in this desolate place has cracked the pitcher and sanity is seeping out.'

Silah came back bearing a large earthenware jug and two pewter mugs; these she placed on the table, then went and seated herself by the fire, where she took up a work basket and began to darn a grey woollen sock. Evans spoke without turning his head.

'Silah, heed this. It seems we have forgotten our guest is a noble lord, a tosspot of George the Regent no less, and he would have you.'

The faintest suspicion of a smile played round Silah's lips, but she did not speak, only continued to darn the sock, and Dunwilliam turned savagely on Evans.

'Keep your foul mouth shut, man.'

Evans chuckled, twisting his face into a parody of a leer.

'Goodness, you must be a smooth-talking lot when you sit boozing with fat Prinny. When George the Regent is about to deflower a girl young enough to be his daughter, how does the royal tongue make known his august desire?' Evans raised his voice to a high-pitched tone. ' 'Tis a great honour I be doing her and make no mistake about it, and if she is that lucky, maybe she'll drop my noble bastard before the leaves fall.'

Dunwilliam was about to leap from his chair and fasten his great hands about the tormentor's neck, when from a long way off came the sound of a hunting horn. It was so faint, yet so very clear, and Evans fell back in his chair, the sneer wiped from his face by an expression of abject terror. Dunwilliam looked from father to daughter with growing astonishment.

'What ails you? It's only someone lost in the snow.'

Evans ignored him, and turned his fear-stricken face towards Silah.

'You'll not go out tonight, and you'll not encourage him to come nigh the house.'

Silah did not answer but continued to work, only now there was a distinct smile parting her lips.

'You'll not go out,' Evans roared, 'but stay at home and respect your father's wishes, or I'll set up a fiery cross on the hill-side and the devil take the consequences.'

The horn sounded again, only now it was nearer, and it was followed by the deep baying of hounds. Dunwilliam strode to the door and was about to pull back the great iron bolts when Evans's fear-hoarse voice reached him.

'Don't open the door. For pity's sake, man, don't open the door.'

Dunwilliam spun round and took in the scene with one

swift glance; Evans was slumped in his chair, terror having wiped away the stern lines from his face, while the girl sat darning, still smiling gently as though blissfully aware she had nothing to fear. Dunwilliam addressed her.

'Who is it that put the fear of Satan into him, and, more to the point, who rides with the hounds in the midst of a snow storm?'

She rose, put the work basket to one side, then looked down at her father.

'If I do not go out to him, he will come knocking at the door, and the hounds will murder your sleep.'

Evans spoke from between clenched teeth.

'Go out then, and be damned to you. But in the name of heaven don't let me see his face.'

She took down a long black cloak from a hook by the fire-place, then walked slowly towards the door. Dunwilliam, determined she would recognise his existence, did not move, and she stopped before his great form, which entirely blocked the doorway.

'You shall not go out to him,' he growled, 'whoever, whatever, he might be.'

Her head came up and he gazed into those wonderful eyes; her voice was soft, as calm as water in moonlight.

'It matters not to me, sir, for if I do not go out, he will surely come in to fetch me, and it might go ill with you.'

'Let him come in,' Dunwilliam muttered. 'He will find one greater than your father.'

The baying of hounds was growing louder by the minute, and the horn shrieked an ear-splitting call that seemed to wake the wind from its sleep, for it suddenly dealt the house a mighty buffet, making windows rattle. Evan ap Evans slid to the floor.

'You best see to my father,' the girl said. 'It seems he has fainted.'

'You're a cold baggage, or are you so hot for the horn-blower there is no warmth left for anyone else?'

The hornblast now seemed but a few feet behind the closed

door, and a series of snorting gasps intermingled with low whines were moving round the house, while the wind sang a mournful dirge as it pleaded for entrance at window frames and chimney pots.

'When I open the door,' Silah said, 'do not, if you value your life, look out, but go to my father and reassure him.'

'If you can look upon he who waits out there,' Dunwilliam moved with great reluctance to one side, 'why can't I?'

The girl's smile was now mocking, taunting him, so that he had great difficulty in keeping his hands idle.

'He will not love *you.*'

She opened the door, and with a shriek of triumph the wind rushed in, tore across the room and made the fire dance a mad reel of terror. Evans groaned and tried to sit up as Dunwilliam slammed the door and moved over to him, looking down with contempt at the white face and trembling hands of the prostrate Welshman. In his world a man did not, whatever his innermost feeling might be, admit to, or display signs of fear. He nudged Evans with his foot.

'Get up, and try to behave like a man.'

The scorn in his voice acted like a whiplash. Evans scrambled to his feet, and pointed a finger that was not yet steady at the Englishman.

'Indeed, it is easy to be brave before you have tasted the acid fruit of terror. Had you gone out there, man, aye, if you had come face to face with – him – and his pack, I've no doubt you'd be singing a different song now.'

'Damnation hell, who is out there?'

'Arawn,' Evans whispered the name; seemed to spit it out as though it were some foul taste. 'Arawn and his pack – the Cwn Annwn.'

'What gibberish is this?' Dunwilliam was aware that a chill had entered his bloodstream, and the knowledge made his anger grow. 'Who is Arawn and the Cwn . . .?'

'Cwn Annwn – the Dogs of Hell, and he rides behind them. 'Tis said he was once king of all the southern regions, but whatever he was once, one thing is sure now, he does not breathe air.'

'A ghost!' Dunwilliam's roar of derision was louder than he intended, for there was a veritable bedlam of sound from behind the closed door; an almost obscene whimpering and howling, a snuffling and padding of great paws. Once the door shook as though some vast body had been hurled against it. 'A ghost king and his phantom hounds? Do you believe that, man?'

'Phantoms!' Evan ap Evans glared at the door, his teeth bared in a maniac grin. 'Mentioned I phantoms? 'Tis no ghosts that go streaking across the moors, 'tis no phantoms that tear a man limb from limb, pull out his windpipe, then chase his soul into the underworld. Demons maybe, half fleshed, half – something, I know not what. Merciful God, if they were only wraiths that go howling through the night, I would sleep peacefully in my bed and smile in the morning.'

'But the girl, your own daughter?' Dunwilliam shook his head, clinging desperately to his disbelief. 'Why is she out there if what you say is true?'

'You must be blind, or stupid,' Evans began, when suddenly, as though a switch had been turned off, the sounds ceased. The silence was broken only by the spluttering fire, and the muffled crash as a pile of snow slid down from the roof.

'The weather is on the turn,' remarked Evans in a matter-of-fact tone of voice.

Dunwilliam rushed to the door and flung it open; outside it had ceased to snow, and there was a vast carpet of whiteness that stretched out under a full moon to the distant mountains. Silah turned as he came out, and for a full minute they stood looking at each other. The girl's eyes were bright and for the first time she seemed to be alive.

'So you are not made of ice. You have a lover who cleverly disguises himself as a bogyman to frighten the wits out of that poor fool in there. How does he do it? Eh? Bang a fir branch against door and windows, howl like a dog on heat, snuffle like a pig in labour? No doubt he has a first-hand knowledge of these things.'

'As you can see, sir,' the girl said quietly, 'there is no one here.'

'Aye, he made a smooth getaway, I'll say that for him.'

He looked around; the snow, apart from his own footprints and the girl's, was smooth and untrampled.

'Or was there anyone at all?'

He reached out and pulled her towards him; he was trembling, found difficulty in breathing.

'What game are you playing? Does he blow his horn out there as a signal for you to come out and put on your performance for Master Bumpkin, your father? Aye, is that it?'

'I must go in, sir,' she murmured softly, 'for there is much to be done, and I would be up early tomorrow.'

'And I would pluck you from this rude earth.' He pressed her slender form to his body, and she was as light as a snowflake, and when he brutally clamped his mouth to hers it was as though he had embraced a statue. With surprising strength she twisted, then ducked under his encircling arms and ran into the house. When he followed a few minutes later, Dunwilliam found her clearing the table; Evan ap Evans was smiling, a sly, almost triumphant smirk.

'You belong to the damned,' he said. 'Before the sun rises you will pray for death, and your prayers will not be answered.'

'Whatever happens,' Dunwilliam spoke quietly, 'I will not run from shadows, nor fall to my knees when a dog barks. Fear makes cowards.'

'Yes, indeed,' Evans nodded, 'and that is why you will go down why I still walk upright. Only fools or heroes stand still when fear warns them they should run, and I, being you understand no gentleman, will crawl on my belly, if by so doing I can breathe a little longer and count the fingers on my right hand.'

'If you are so frightened of what you imagine exists out there,' Dunwilliam jerked his head in the direction of the door, 'why don't you run from this place? The world is large.'

'Because the moors are my father and mother, and if I do not rebel my few sheep grow fat, my crops, such as they are, stand erect, untouched by blight or frost, and sometimes there is a gold coin on the doorstep. Kings have always rewarded the fathers of their mistresses.'

'And madmen can sometimes contaminate those who are nearest to them,' said Dunwilliam caustically. 'It is time someone removed her from your company.'

Evan ap Evans laughed, a great bellowing roar, and the girl drew near and stood watching him, her face grave, her eyes dark mirrors that gave no hint of the thoughts lurking behind them. Presently, when her father had recovered from his outburst, she touched his shoulder.

'It is time you went to your room, for I must make up a bed for him before the fire.'

'Sleep, aye,' he grinned with almost childish joy. 'Let him sleep while he may, for tomorrow . . .' He stopped, and the smile died. 'But I will weep for him.'

He went quietly to his room, and Dunwilliam watched Silah bolt the door. He smiled grimly.

'Thank you for locking him in. I will sleep all the better for knowing that madman cannot come out.'

Silah took a pile of blankets out of a heavy oak chest.

'He would not sleep at all if I did not lock him in. There are bars on his window.'

'He indeed fears your bogyman,' Dunwilliam sneered.

'He has the courage of his fears,' the girl said softly as she laid cushions on the floor and covered them with a blanket. 'There, you should sleep soundly enough.' She walked towards what Dunwilliam assumed to be her bedroom, then paused. 'Lord Dunwilliam, I will give you a piece of advice which you can disregard if you wish. Do not, under any circumstances, leave the house before morning. Despite what my father said, I think you are safe, so long as you do not leave this room and are prepared to depart at daybreak.'

'I am indeed flattered by your concern.'

She shook her head.

'I am not concerned, but I would rather not have your blood on my head.'

She went into her room, then closed the door.

When Dunwilliam woke the fire had sunk down to a black pile of charred logs, and the room had surrendered to a bone-chilling cold that made him pull the blankets tighter about him. He had awoken suddenly, been jerked back into consciousness by a sound, and for a while he lay motionless, trying to remember what it had been. A log settled in the grate, a pile of snow slid from the roof, a floorboard creaked as the change in temperature made it expand. Even as Dunwilliam pondered on the problem, the sound came again. The distant blast of a horn: clear, unmistakable, a raucous call that drove the last residue of sleep from Dunwilliam's head, and made him stare with wide-open eyes across the darkened room. A door opened, soft footsteps slowly crossed the room, paused by the recumbent man then moved on. The bolts on the front door were carefully drawn back; a blast of colder air caressed Dunwilliam's hair, then the door closed and he was alone.

The lust, the anger, the great desire to possess, to snatch from another that what must be his; the overwhelming need to hurt, strike, smash, rend, all this and more, drove him from the makeshift bed, sent him blundering round the room in search of his greatcoat and hat, then out into the moon-painted night.

He found his horse in an out-house, and he saddled it with cold-numb fingers, cursing, mouthing foul obscenities, but all the while he was fired by a fierce excitement. She was out on the moor, on her way to meet some fool with a horn, and now she was legitimate prey for he who rode the fastest.

Lord Dunwilliam swung himself up into the saddle and rode forth in all his strength, for he was armed with pride, certain that defeat or disappointment would never face him; the brutal, animal courage of his kind sat cheek by jowl with pride and together they supported his arrogant commonsense, which would reject any object between heaven and earth that had not been accepted by one or more of his five senses.

He followed the girl's trail easily enough, for the imprint of her small feet had been perfectly retained by the smooth carpet of snow, and presently he caught sight of her black-clad figure making for the mountain slopes. The distance between them narrowed, and she must have known who followed, but her head did not turn, and she continued to trudge onward as though certain that nothing could impede her journey. He spurred his horse forward so that plumes of powdered snow sprang up around its hoofs, then he was riding abreast of her, looking down on the graceful figure that even the voluminous cloak could not hide.

'You cannot escape me,' he said, and the joy that sang in his blood was a wondrous thing. 'Your horn-blowing bumpkin must hunt another quarry tonight.'

She spoke without looking up.

'Ride north and you will be safe, but for your own sake come no farther.'

'We will both ride north,' he said, and bending down he gripped her under the armpits and pulled the light form up on to the saddle. She did not struggle, but relaxed back in his arms with a tiny sigh of resignation, and the pale, flawless face was as unrevealing as the eternal hills. Lord Dunwilliam wheeled his horse about and began to wend his way towards the distant lake that lay like a silver salver in the bright moonlight. The hot madness flooded his being, and he was as a god before whom elements bow, and he poured out a torrent of words that demanded no answer. They were but an outlet for his great joy.

'You shall have dresses to caress your soft whiteness, and diamonds to kiss the velvet sheen of your neck, and I shall bring the great ones of the earth to pay you homage, the nobles, the word-builders, even Prinny himself. But perhaps not, perhaps not. Why should I reveal your beauty to lustful eyes? Maybe I'll build you a cage of gold, a fortress manned by an army of one, and together we will keep the world at bay. I'll teach you to smile, then wait for that great day when you will laugh, and my love – yes, my love, will light a fire that will consume us both, and each night we will die of ecstasy, to be reborn when the sun . . .'

The words ceased to flow, he looked down at the pale face so close to his own; it was still devoid of expression, a beautiful mask, but a single tear ran down either cheek.

'You are crying,' he whispered. 'You must not cry.'

'I am sad for you,' she said.

'For me?'

There was a slight inclination of her head.

'Yes, in the same way that I would be sad for any living creature doomed to unthinkable horror.'

He tilted her head with his free hand and there was a strange gentleness in his voice.

'You silly, superstitious child, what tricks has your horn-blowing peasant been playing?' Do you suppose I would be frightened by an oaf on horseback and a few mangy hounds? In a few hours we will be in Bala – there I'll hire a coach for London.'

She shook her head. 'You cannot escape. Even now he is on the move, marshalling his pack for the great chase. When the horn sounds, and the hounds are in full cry, you will not know east from west, or be certain where the sky meets the earth. There will be sadness in my heart when you go down before his wrath, but when it is over, and the snow has hidden that which must not be seen, then I will forget you for ever. It will be as if you had never existed.'

The anger, which had lain like a wounded beast far back in the dark caverns of his brain, reared up, and he growled:

'I promise you, wench, you will have no reason to forget me. You may fear me, hate me, but you will never forget.'

Suddenly he reined in and looked back over one shoulder. The horn blast was distinct, but even more clear was the deep baying of many hounds, and there appeared on the distant mountainside a pack of swift-moving creatures that glittered bright red in the cold moonlight. For a moment Dunwilliam doubted the evidence presented by his eyes. They had seemingly sprung out of nowhere, a grim, nightmare pack that were streaking straight for him, eating up the distance, and behind them rode the dread horseman. Both rider and horse were of gigantic stature, and the man, if indeed such a creature could be so called, wore a great black cloak that streamed out behind him like some monstrous wing.

Dunwilliam used his spurs, but they were not necessary, for the horse was terrified. It leapt forward, ploughing up the snow as it desperately tried to outrun the grim pack, but the going was hard and Dunwilliam found he had lost all sense of direction. Behind him he heard the snuffling, howling, grotesque baying that at times ascended into an unearthly shriek, and no matter how fast Lucifer ran, the sounds grew louder, the impossible which Dunwilliam still refused to accept was closing in. At last he knew flight was futile, and he had little stomach for being the hunted, chased like a fox for a madman's pleasure, so he guided the near-exhausted horse towards a solitary tree and prepared to face the inevitable.

He dismounted, then dragged the girl down beside him and she leant against the tree, calm, her beauty a cold flame, and even now Dunwilliam wanted to feast his eyes on that pale face, but the baying, howling pack would not be denied and he was aware that the horse, relieved of its double burden, was a black streak, flying across the snow.

They were bright red, glittering as though encased in scarlet armour. They fanned out and formed a half-circle, still moving in, but slowly now, a few inches at a time, eyes gleaming like hot coals, whimpering with awful anticipation, and as they drew nearer Dunwilliam realised what gave them that awesome red sheen. They were covered with blood. Gore coated the great bodies, flowed down the long ears, oozed out of the drooling mouths, but the snow around them was virgin white, and Dunwilliam swallowed his fear, drove it down into his stomach, where it lay like a block of frozen acid.

The great horseman sat motionless amid his fearsome pack, his face in deep shadow cast by the cowl which masked his head, and Silah sighed, and Dunwilliam saw the light which transformed her eyes into pools of wondrous joy, saw the smile which lit up her face, saw the delicate flush that tinted the smooth cheeks.

'This is what you want?' he asked.

'He is the earth, the hills,' she nodded slowly. 'His breath is the wind that holds dominion over the frozen moors, his strength comes from the rocks and bubbling streams and his soul is born of darkness and moonlight. How could I not love him?'

The Hounds of Hell were nearer; their bellies touched the snow, the blood-coated hides seethed and bubbled, and the wings of the half-circle were folding, closing in, while the black horseman sat motionless, neither he nor his horse betraying the slightest flicker of life. Lord Dunwilliam raised his voice.

'Hear me, Arawn, whatever you are, I do not accept you nor the blood-soaked filth that surrounds you. You are born of ignorance, stupidity, the child of crazed brains, and I curse you. Get down to the hell which is rightfully yours, or go and frighten babies or old men in their cups, but leave an intelligent, educated man in peace. Set those – things on me if you can, but so long as I can speak, see, or even think, I will deny your existence.'

Silah moved to his side, then reaching up she placed one arm around his neck and pulled his head down. She kissed him full on the lips and at last fear began to uncoil like a cold snake.

'You are worthy to follow him,' she said, then her arm dropped away and she began to walk towards the approaching pack, straight for the black horseman. As she passed the nearest Hell Hound she patted its blood-coated head, and it whimpered, while a dripping tongue flicked out to lick her dainty hand. When she at last reached the great horse another hound crouched down so that she could use it as a mounting block, and presently she was nestling against that black breast, one great arm was about her slim waist, and she was the dream girl who had found joy in a nightmare. The hounds came closer, but now their movements were slightly faster. The blood seemed to flow more freely, and Dunwilliam crossed himself, tried to remember the Church dogma, but his brain was being slowly paralysed by the rising fear.

'In the name of the Father, the Son and the Holy Ghost, I command you to go from hence . . .'

The girl smiled; she was now a spectator who knew how the play was to end, and was perhaps a little bored.

Dunwilliam was back against the tree, his eyes dilated, sweat pouring down his congested face, but to the very end he fought back in the only way he knew.

'Merciful God, give me the gift of disbelief, strengthen my doubt, let me see only reality . . .'

The first hound leapt, and its blood-soaked head filled the universe; the gleaming eyes became a fire-walled hell from which there was no escape, and there was a mighty pain in Dunwilliam's throat. Then they came in from all directions, snarling, fighting for their share of the threshing body, and Silah's soft laughter was like the wind playing with summer grass.

He came up from the hell where pain and terror reigned and lay still for a few minutes, trying to understand. The pain had gone, fear was dying, and he felt strong, alert, but the stench of corruption was all around, sweet and cloying, and he knew he was covered with blood. The hounds had torn his soul from his body and he was soaked in a warm wetness. It salted his tongue, filled his nostrils with a sweet essence, and it was good. Life-giving.

The hounds had withdrawn. They sat watching him, silent, still, and He who sat on the great horse with his arm about the starry-eyed girl had pulled back his cowl so that Lord Dunwilliam was able to see the face. Dark, awful, evil, beautiful. He thought of a black serpent, the towering mountains, the terror that lurks in unlighted rooms, then looked again on the face of Arawn, and surrendered to a wave of fawning, self-effacing love. He crawled forward on his belly, eased his way through the motionless hounds and at last came to rest by the great hoofs. The terrible eyes looked down at him, and Silah nodded gently as though well pleased by the turn of events. Then Arawn swung his horse round, raised a black horn to his lips and the mighty blast rang out. The Hell Hounds sprang to instant death-tainted life, began to snort, snuffle and make the night hideous with their deep-throated growls, then the great horse leapt forward and the blood-coated pack streaked after it, eager for the next victim, knowing that soon the sun would drive darkness from the black steel sky.

Dunwilliam watched them go, indecision confusing his thoughts, but aware of a great longing to – what? To hate, to see terror come to life on a complacent face, to hear screams, to rend, to devour? Arawn and the Cwn Annwn stopped some hundred yards ahead and He looked back before sounding another arrogant blast on his horn. Lord Dunwilliam knew what he must do.

He climbed up on to his four feet, shook his blood-soaked hide, then streaked forth to join the pack.

Ngaio Marsh

'The finest writer in the English language of the pure, classical, puzzle whodunit. Among the Crime Queens, Ngaio Marsh stands out as an Empress.' *Sun*. 'Her work is as near flawless as makes no odds: character, plot, wit, good writing and sound technique.' *Sunday Times*. 'The brilliant Ngaio Marsh ranks with Agatha Christie and Dorothy Sayers.' *Times Literary Supplement*.

Last Ditch

Vintage Murder

Death and the Dancing Footman

Death at the Dolphin

Hand in Glove

Colour Scheme

Scales of Justice

Singing in the Shrouds

Spinsters in Jeopardy

A Clutch of Constables

Death in a White Tie

Dead Water